THE

DESERT ANGLER

Nikolai Gorski

THE

DESERT ANGLER

March 2012

The Queen Creek Press

Phoenix

A Creative Beans R&D LLC Book
Published by The Queen Creek Press

Copyright © 2012 By Creative Beans R&D LLC
All rights reserved under International and Pan-American Copyright Conventions.
Published in the United States by
Creative Beans R&D LLC dba The Queen Creek Press.

ISBN: 978-0-615-54263-8

Cover art by Neil Coyne

Manufactured in the United States of America

Acknowledgements

The author gratefully acknowledges his wife and kids for filling his life with tremendous love, immense pride, and infectious joy; Neil Coyne for the cover art; Thomas E. Sheridan for his book Arizona, A History; Mark Kurlansky for his book Salt, A World History; Edith Hamilton for her book Mythology; Elizabeth for her editorial excellence, great suggestions, and keen eye; and a particular oversized plastic blue fish for the idea.

CHAPTERS

Lightning..1

Thunder...17

Rain..35

Surge...47

Hail...59

Calm..79

Two Twisters..91

Stillness...103

Storm Front...115

Monsoon...129

Tsunami...149

Aftermath..159

Fresh Kill...181

Hurricane...197

Firestorm...211

Gale..225

The Desert Angler...................................239

THE

DESERT ANGLER

LIGHTNING

"The correct term is mounted, ma'am." New to the neighborhood, Colonel Gunnar Wiley, Retired, stood proudly in his driveway amidst three First Ladies of Rancho Opulente. His Hawaiian orange shirt decorated beautifully with large white orchids did little to hide his large stomach. But his kind smile and smooth sound diverted attention away from his soft-centered echelon. His new female friends immediately hung on his every word.

"Well, it looks stuffed to me," teased Mrs. Florence.

"Professional taxidermists take offense to their works of wild game art being characterized by the untrained eye as stuffed," Colonel Wiley said with his genteel-sounding Southern accent. "It's not actually stuffed. It's a replica made from a mold taken of the fish by the taxidermist. And then he paints it to match the original coloration."

"It's so big!" Mrs. Andersen winked at Mrs. Florence as they circled a long wooden crate lying in the street.

"Took me only three hours to reel 'im in! Broke both the length and weight record at the dock down in Cabo. Got the pictures to prove it. Here, look!" From his wallet, he pushed at them a small photo of him and a fish. "The Mexicans on the boat named him Lightning 'cause o' the way he hit the line like a big bolt of lightning." The handwritten sign in the photo read, "14 feet, 4 inches, 1,265 lbs."

"I'm grillin' swordfish tonight. You're all cordially invited."

Everyone laughed hysterically, while he was serious. Along with his life-sized stuffed trophy, he shipped hundreds of pounds of swordfish and had no place to put it—or for that matter, any real desire to eat it. He hated the gamey taste. *But what the hell, he caught the damn thing.*

No one in the neighborhood could ignore the spectacle. During the past couple of months, the ritual of new homebuyers moving into the brand-new Rancho Opulente, Arizona, neighborhood became commonplace. But the colonel and his fourteen-foot crated fish sitting in the middle of the street certainly made the day and begged for attention.

"Tacky," Mrs. Florence whispered under her breath while looking down to compare her French pedicure to the rest of the circle's bumble-gum toes. She wasn't the only one looking at open-toed sandals and silky feet. The colonel always wore aviator glasses to hide his wandering eyes. He salivated.

The small crowd gathered in the street in front of a large, brightly colored moving van with polished black tires and shining wheels. On the side of the truck's trailer, a desert mural depicted an early twentieth-century gritty Arizona Territory Ranger atop an equally tough grey horse. Both looked down from a wind-weathered, flat-topped mountain into a valley through which a black steam engine locomotive puffed black smoke as it pulled into a prosperous future with copper oar pellets that filled a hundred crackling railcars. Giant green saguaro cactus filled the trailer's mural. The name "Pearl" decorated the truck's mud flaps. Bram Hoogeveen, the Hercules Moving Company proprietor, had rescued the old gal from the junkyard. He had lovingly restored her into a customized pearl colored "low-rider" truck. Its soft brown leather seats matched the mahogany steering wheel and gear shifter. Bram meticulously kept her clean with the aid of several instruments, including a toothbrush and toothpick.

While the condition of the truck exceeded any standard, Bram's health did not. He stood next to the truck staring at a clipboard. On his forehead, small eagle wing tattoos replaced his shaved eyebrows. The ink in his skin appeared cheap, the artwork quick. His stance looked uncomfortable, his frail body broken. On that day, he suffered from dysentery. The truck driver ignored the activity occurring on the opposite side of his precious Pearl.

Meanwhile, the mightiest of the moving men, forty-two-year-old Karl Hoogeveen (Bram's younger brother), grunted as he—by himself—loaded upon his back a huge, thick, oak-framed leather couch. He used straps and his in-depth knowledge of fulcrums, levers, and physics to gracefully balance and move mountains. He wore dockworker navy-blue pants, exotic-looking European work boots, and a thick, expensive, heavy starch-pressed white T-shirt—stained with sweat and dust from the job. His years of experience taught him that the woman of the house always watched him work. He always wore expensive clothes and changed his shirts often during the day. *A woman's first impression was everything.* His big upper arm, large legs, and massive chest all flexed and twitched as he walked, smiling, with a several-hundred-pound couch on his back on display for the ladies. He smelled the potpourri of pretty scents coming from them. Mrs. Florence noticed the anchor tattoo on his left arm swinging with the movement of his bulging bicep. His platinum prosthetic right arm did not deter from the Greek god's presence. All the Opulente First Ladies started to feel a little bit viscous.

"How does he do that?" Mrs. Florence asked.

"As I was saying..." the colonel interrupted.

Capricious Jo Harmony (C.J.) observed quietly with her big zircon eyes and intuition. Karl seemed familiar to her. But she wasn't sure. *It had to be him. His missing arm. What were the chances it could be someone else? It had to be him!* Then the memory of the past came into her as quickly and forcefully as Lightning hitting the bait on the colonel's fishing line. *It was Karl.* The past pulled at her. Jerked her. Tore into her. Deeply. And ripped her out of a tranquil sea into an unfamiliar atmosphere of emotion. She fought against the line's pull. She tried to remain calm and in control. But could not.

Meanwhile, the other women conversed among themselves about Karl. Their judgment told them that it was absolutely ludicrous to get all worked up about a man. They knew a guy like Karl attracted every woman with whom he came in contact. Each refused to be just another pretty face to any man—including Karl. But their obstinate pride conflicted with their true hidden desires.

As the other women contemplated Karl, C.J.'s confusion continued. She tried to end her uncomfortable feelings. She ran her deep-bougainvillea-colored fingernails through her bundle of beautiful cinnabar-brown curls. Looked at herself through her little leopard-skin-colored compact kit. Puckered her brilliant lips. And applied her favorite glossy lipstick.

"Aren't you afraid that he is going to drop that couch? Why don't you all go and make sure he doesn't break anything?" Striking, C.J. teased the others.

"Yes. Yes." Mrs. Anderson thought it was a great idea to go watch Karl. This was no joke. "Let's go see," she said.

In a flash the ladies all followed in amazement to watch the Scandinavian-looking, blond-haired hunk move a couch. Karl smiled. Then he pierced Mrs. Andersen with his remarkable turquoise-colored eyes. C.J. grew angry and perhaps jealous of flirty Mrs. Andersen. *She was such a tramp.* The colonel turned to inspect the inventory sheet with the truck driver. The driver's dysentery bleached his skin to the color of an opal buried beneath the desert.

C.J. only thought about Karl. Bram shyly stared at her from behind his big resting rig. She did not recognize him. Bram's look had changed dramatically from his appearance as a young man when she had known him. She perceived him as a meek, aging, moving man peering at her through two sad eyes.

Scratching his head, the colonel realized that the big blue fish might not fit into the house. While the grand entranceway presented ample space for visitors and new furniture, the hall leading to the trophy room may not have been so spacious.

"We'll have to pass it through the window straight into the trophy room," said the truck driver. "We'll remove the window. Not to worry." As he spoke, he looked at C.J. He recognized her. He did not even hear himself speak.

The colonel looked bewildered. *But the moving men seemed OK. Karl seemed to know what he was doing.* "Alright. Full steam ahead. Take off the window." The colonel gave the order.

While Karl and his two colossal companions worked together to pry the window away from its frame, the colonel turned his attention to the beauties before him. He reached into his shirt pocket and withdrew a small white cigarette. With an old worn brass lighter engraved with an Army Green Beret insignia and the words "Vietnam 1967" on it, Colonel Wiley lit his cigarette and puffed a cloud of smoke into the air. A light breeze gently pushed the fume into the breathing space of the entire circle. Mrs. Andersen inhaled. She liked the smell. It reminded her of many good times in the past. The bars she used to frequent. The topless rides in river speedboats. The motor sports in the desert. And the men she used to meet. It had been so long since she had been out like that. She missed those days. Then she settled into Saturday soccer and Sunday backyard pool parties. She guessed it wasn't so bad. *She could have married somebody poor. She had done pretty good.*

"That's Capricious over there, Karl." Bram had limped over to Karl by the colonel's window.

"What? Where?" The muscles in Karl's face dropped.

"Over there! Look!" Bram pointed.

"How did I not see her? She was standing right there the whole time!" With his left hand, he clasped his head. He looked at Bram. "What should I do?"

"I dunno." Bram looked down in shame at the newly installed green turf upon which they both stood.

"Maybe we ought to go in the house. Anybody for a Bloody Mary?" The colonel spoke through the side of his mouth while he puffed his cigarette.

"It's not too early. It's eleven a.m. I say we go for it!" Mrs. Florence read Mrs. Andersen's mind.

The colonel turned to C.J.

"How 'bout you, pretty lady?"

C.J. thought about it. She tried to remember the last time she had drunk an alcoholic beverage. *Was it five months ago at New Year's?*

"Maybe you prefer margaritas?" The sun reflected off the rim of the colonel's aviators and caught C.J. in the eye.

"Have a margarita and a Bloody Mary!" The colonel gave her a wink.

"What the hell!"

From a distance, Karl watched C.J among the crowd of ladies while his moving mates fiddled with the window. He looked upon these women as a garden of scented flowers. His floral delight, C.J., proved prettier than all the rest. He watched as coy C.J. kept a knowing grin while the others gossiped. She confidently stared everyone in the eye. Her huge zircon eyes, pleasant but serious smile, and bushy brown hair weakened anyone in her gaze. Mrs. Andersen, Mrs. Florence, and yes, even Colonel Wiley melted before her. The colonel tried to be cute with his "Margarita and a Bloody Mary." But ultimately he fell prey to her silent spell.

While conversing, the three ladies kept noticing Karl. They watched his body movements—his behavior and mannerisms. Karl, though, never permitted them to see him looking back at them. He knew women hated rubbernecking male swine. He appeared to the women to be engaged in serious thought—something outside the moment. The window and its frame kept him merely annoyed with the two other movers. They happily took direction from Karl, relieving him of any real burden, permitting him to focus on the color, sound, and scent filling the world in front of the house.

The group, with laughter and joy, walked toward the door to the house. And finally Karl's eyes met C.J.'s. Neither of the two flinched or grinned. They just coldly stared deep into each other's eyes. This was not fun or polite or flirtatious. This hurt because their shared memory opened old wounds. For the length of the walk up and into the house, Karl and C.J. exchanged searing sincerity beneath the desert sun. After she passed through the doorway, King Karl knelt to the ground. Her presence had completely overwhelmed him. Inside, C.J. wiped light tears from her eyes. Neither could speak. No one noticed.

Dizzy, Karl walked over to a water jug and dumped its contents upon his sweaty self. Then he rested in the shade. The other two men declared the removal of the window, and the semi-truck driver, Bram, asked them to pass the fish through the open space. Karl's manual labor was done for the day. The swordfish was the last item to be moved into the house.

Inside the house, the crowd conversed.

"I hear you rarely get bad hair days out here in the desert!" The colonel's wife, twenty years younger than the colonel, entered the kitchen. The countertops were sticky with Vodka and mixer.

"Everyone, this is Caroline." The colonel handed her an extra spicy Bloody Mary with two celery sticks and lots of celery leaves—just the way she liked her wake-up call.

"But my friends call me Ace," she said in a raspy voice.

She combed her still-wet hair. Though freshly showered, she still reeked of stale alcohol, cigarettes, and marijuana. A little toke in the morning always took the edge off a hangover. The Wileys had arrived the night before in order to be at the house upon the movers' arrival. The whites of Caroline's eyes looked pale yellow, and the whites of her teeth charcoal grey. Caroline flicked the lengthy ash of her cigarette into the sink. The colonel stood next to her, loading up the blender with more fun. The ceiling above pounded and knocked with Caroline's three illegitimate teenagers jumping around upstairs. Caroline and the colonel had only met a couple of years before. Loud annoying music clashed against the screaming blender. C.J. examined the historic scratches and stains on the electronic mixer.

"I think we're gonna like livin' here!" The colonel's cigarette bounced up and down in his mouth. A little ash fell into the blender. *What the hell? Leave it. It's all good.*

"Caroline," the colonel continued, "a package arrived this morning. I had it sent to the new address."

The colonel shut off the blender. Poured its contents into several large glasses and added pepper, Tabasco sauce, two large celery sticks with the leaves still intact, and a couple of ice cubes.

He headed out the back sliding door to the patio bordering the Olympic-size pool. He returned with a wooden box in his hand. Cored large round holes ventilated each side. The words "Live Animal" decorated its top. He placed the box on the kitchen counter.

"Anyone for a Bloody Mary? Hurry up now. Everyone should have one before the big show!"

In turn each of the houseguests received a brunch-time drink in preparation for the mysterious performance.

"So what's in the box?" Mrs. Anderson was not shy.

Caroline replied, "A box turtle."

The crowd roared with laughter.

"A box turtle?"

"We had 'er delivered all the way from Billings, Montana," Caroline continued. "I met this guy online, and he paid us a stud fee to board his female turtle for a few weeks."

"I don't get it," Mrs. Florence interjected.

"Our turtle, Chester, is in back of the house. We figured he was getting lonely. We've had him for years. He's never had a little honey—if you know what I mean." The colonel smirked.

"So we're gonna watch Chester do it with that girl turtle?"

"Her name is Matilda. And yes. Right after Colonel mixes up another round of drinks." Caroline bit off a chunk of her celery stick and chewed it with her mouth open, smacking her lips.

C.J. shook her head in disbelief. No one knew she still thought of Karl. The colonel began concocting more liquid.

"So what do your husbands do on a beautiful Saturday such as this?" asked Colonel Wiley.

"They do what we tell them to do!" Mrs. Andersen replied.

The women all stood around looking at one another with all-knowing looks of approval, except Mrs. Florence. She looked at her soft leather sandals and admired her pedicure. She felt no need to boss around her husband. She enjoyed making him happy. The daily adoring attention he gave to her lulled her into subtle submission. Colonel Wiley sipped from his glass. The celery stalk tickled his ear. He lifted one thin eyebrow as his attention grew.

"You don't say!"

"You betcha!" Mrs. Andersen continued, "Right now Charles should be just about finishing up folding the laundry and getting ready to drive our daughter, Samantha—she's nine—to her soccer game. Then he'll be off to the store to pick up this week's groceries."

"You're kiddin' me."

"No. I'm serious. He is a very liberated man."

"Well, I'd call it something else!" The colonel added another shot of vodka to his Bloody Mary.

"What's wrong with a man helping out with the chores around the house?" C.J. spoke up.

"It's woman's work."

"What do you mean?"

"It's woman's work. Plain and simple!"

The colonel knew he was beginning to get under their skin.

"I don't do that crap! I don't lift a finger. I make all the big decisions, and that's it."

"That's because you hired Maria the housekeeper to do all of that stuff." Caroline was beginning to slur her words as she finished up her second drink.

"Regardless," the colonel fought back. "I do not and never have done any women's work in my entire life. That's it." He smiled proudly.

"Do you go to the mall with your wife?" Mrs. Andersen rejoined the exchange.

"When I go to the mall, it's a special guest appearance to make a decision on a purchase. I am there for a reason, a specific purpose. So there."

The rest of the women snickered. C.J. watched Caroline exit the kitchen to the adjacent dining room. She then spied on Caroline through the reflection in a mirror leaning up against the wall waiting to be hung. With the aid of her dark red drink, Caroline negotiated a little white pill out of her pocket, into her mouth, and down her throat. Then moments later she returned to the conversation. The muscles in her face had slid, and her eyes became extremely glassed over. A smile refused to leave her countenance.

"Have you scheduled your colonoscopy?" Caroline blurted out as she entered the kitchen.

The people in the room froze, waiting for a response. The colonel ignored Caroline and pretended nothing had been said. But nevertheless, the peacock had been removed from his lofty perch.

"Let's go watch the turtles." Colonel Wiley grabbed the "Live Animal" box and marched out the back door, trying to maintain a military posture despite his belly.

"How about *your* husband, C.J.?" Mrs. Andersen asked a direct question.

C.J. thought about it for a moment.

"Well. When I worked—I used to own my own public relations firm—I had to fight to get him to do anything. Then he would shape up for a while. Then after a couple of weeks, he'd retreat back into his old bad habits. I even went on strike. But during that period, the work wouldn't get done. The kids would suffer. So I decided to stay home. I sold the business."

"You caved in!" Mrs. Andersen scolded.

"No. No. I did not cave in. I made sacrifices for the benefit of my children. I did it because I love my kids."

"But now he is in control. He controls you."

"I assure you, that's not the case."

"But as long as he has power of the purse, he controls you."

"*I am in control.*" C.J.'s upper lip stiffened, and the shape of her eyes changed from doe to Bengal tiger.

THUNDER

MARCH 1974

Bonito Pablo Flores ("Paul"), a second-generation Mexican-American, pulled up to his humble middle-class home. His wife, peeking through the window, barely recognized the dull *palo verde* color of his desert-dust-covered United States Border Patrol car. The Arizona wind had kicked up during the day, forcing Paul to use the windshield wipers to dry wipe the dust off the car's windshield.

Paul's wife, Emily, knew he loved his job. From hooking his badge upon his muscular chest, to buckling his gun belt around his forty-five-inch waist, he greeted each day with confidence and enthusiasm. At the time he had just begun his second week of K-9 unit training and knew he had found his calling.

As Paul opened the door and stepped out from the front seat, the listing car righted. His three hundred pounds relieved the newly replaced shock absorbers of their burden. Only Thunder remained in the back. Six foot five Paul bent over and brushed away some dust from the backseat window to assess the one-hundred-forty-pound Caucasian Ovcharka's disposition. Through the clouded window, Paul peered at his new patrol partner in training. The circumference of Thunder's head reminded Paul of the massive brown bear that his father shot up near the Grand Canyon...And of the embarrassment brought by the subsequent poaching conviction. Things were tough enough for immigrant families. Paul committed himself not to fall prey to any situation that could feed stereotypical criticisms from his fellow Americans. He would help President Nixon bring order to the previous decade's unrest.

Thunder growled at Paul.

"Damn!"

Paul suspected he might have a problem on his hands. None of the other officers were brave enough to partner up with Thunder. They understood that some of the dogs, including Thunder, came to the academy from Europe and Russia. Common wisdom assumed that Thunder probably came from an aggressive background. The dog had been bred and trained in Siberia, where he served a year of duty at the notorious Black Dolphin maximum-security prison. After acquiring Thunder, the US Border Patrol K-9 Academy soon discovered that despite his extensive training in Russia, the dog did not have the discipline for any regular crowd control duty or officer patrol. The K-9 experts deemed him best suited for border drug enforcement, limiting his contact with the public.

Days before on the second day of training, Thunder stubbornly refused Paul's instruction. During the incident Paul feared the threat of being released from the K-9 program. He knew that if an officer could not control his dog, the agency would expend neither time nor money on the pair. The members of the academy witnessed Paul's face flash between pale and pink for twenty minutes as he attempted to command Thunder into submission. Finally, after three Hail Marys and an Our Father, Thunder obeyed his master.

Then on the dusty day in front of Paul's home, his new companion exhibited its stubborn mean streak once again. Only Paul's wife knew that Paul wore her mother's rosary underneath his Douglas-fir-green uniform. Looking over the car and through the window, Paul saw Emily wave the Sign of The Cross, press together her petite hands, and look up to the Lord. Paul remembered Sister Miriam and St. Francis.

"Lord, grant me the strength to accept the things I cannot change, the courage to change the things I can, and the wisdom to know the difference."

He believed—well, he hoped–that Thunder he could change. He resigned to join Thunder in the backseat and to force his will upon the dog's. He committed to physical confrontation with the beast.

"O My God, I am heartily sorry for having offended Thee, and I detest all my sins because I dread the loss of Heaven and the pains of Hell; but most of all because they offend Thee, my God, Who art all-good and deserving of all my love. I firmly resolve, with the help of Thy grace, to confess my sins, to do penance, and to amend my life. Amen."

Meanwhile, across the street, a pretty ten-year-old girl named Capricious Jo Harmony rode her sparkling new, metallic, light-blue bicycle. She stored the bike in the living room of her house, as Santa Claus had given her the special bike. The day's outdoor dust had not yet dulled its luster. Her blue and yellow outfit and white shoes matched the bike's hand-painted daffodils and fine pinstripes. She rode in circles aimlessly, singing "London Bridge is falling down. Falling down. Falling down..." Far away were the worries of spelling tests and simple mathematical computation. Instead, while she kept an eye out for oncoming traffic, she thought about the blue sky above the desert dust and about her dainty purse, snugly resting in the bike's wicker white basket. The purple purse clashed with the day's color scheme. She knew her daddy would fix the problem with a new smartly colored purse once she made him aware of the necessity. Daddy never said no.

She rode in and out of neighboring driveways, in and out of the street, and in and out of little Karl Hoogeveen's line of sight. Karl lived next to Paul. Paul lived next to Capricious. Picking his nose, Karl observed both from his porch. Karl heard Thunder growling. He heard Capricious singing. To him, the dog's bass tones and the girl's sopranos synchronized into a peculiar song. The boy closed his eyes and imagined a symphony and a chorus accompanying the sounds of beauty atop those of the beast.

Karl's older brother, Bram, interrupted Karl's thought. A psychedelic-colored surfer-style van driven by a young teenage girl sputtered up to Karl's residence. Bram stepped out of the apartment located above the garage. Wearing no shirt and a pair of jeans short cutoffs, he went out to the van. The girl smiled and handed him a dinner plate. Bram received the food and returned to his cave. The girl waited in the van. Minutes later Bram appeared with a finished plate. He gave it back to her and she departed. Bram turned around and burped.

Both Bram and Karl had been blessed with extremely good looks. At age ten Karl was beginning to become aware of his gift. He noticed girls, and women, staring at him. By age twenty-two, his brother Bram learned to take advantage of his looks.

The reason for the difference in their ages had always been a topic of great speculation. A private woman, their mother, never revealed the sad truth. A sniper in Korea had killed Bram's father. A sniper in Vietnam had killed Karl's father. The boy's mother suffered from a propensity for tough-looking men in the Corps. It was from her stunning looks alone that the boys benefitted.

"That kid hasn't worked a day in his life!" Capricious's father, Don, remarked to his neighbor, Mr. Marks, as he walked down his driveway. He had not noticed Capricious's older sister, Lucy, hiding in the van with the other girl. He had forbidden sixteen-year-old Lucy from hanging around older Bram.

"I only wish I had his looks. Gosh sakes, I can only imagine his life."

It pained both him and his neighbor, Mr. Marks, to witness such raw natural power over the opposite sex. Though each dearly loved his wife, together they shared the lifelong study of unquantifiable female complexities. The pursuit's elusive nature led them to envy and despise young Bram.

The two men's indolent investigation sampled the tiny population of Goodyear, Arizona, where they lived.

Goodyear was a company town. In 1917 a young executive at the Goodyear Tire Company purchased several thousand acres of land in response to the increased demand for rubber tires (and the cotton woven into them) during World War I. The then recently completed Hoover Dam and several other public irrigation projects combined with cheap desert land prices made West Phoenix an attractive location for growing cotton.

After the war had ended and after the wearing deficiencies of natural rubber plant and cotton-threaded tires became apparent, Goodyear, Arizona, morphed into an aerospace and defense industry-based town during World War II and into the Cold War era. Loral Corporation later purchased Goodyear Aerospace. Most of the residents on Don Harmony's street worked as engineers for one of the major defense companies or for one of the smaller contractors. Don Harmony and Michael Marks were no exception.

"I know why you let me sit in the corner!" Don jabbed at Mr. Marks.

The two of them had just been at the corner greasy spoon. They left work early and had intended on a coffee and donut each. The waitress, Karl's mom, Rebekka, easily sold them on marbled eighteen-ounce Angus rib eye. How they intended to explain to their wives' their full bellies and corrugated imaginations remained a mystery. It was not the first time they had faced such a pickle. Their wives were both inside their homes lovingly preparing dinner on the day that the Boston Marathon's running included its first female racers.

The diner, aptly named Harry's Diner, fell into a lucrative business model based on two simple principles—buxom waitresses and pretty good food. Preoccupied engineers wearing white collars and cordovan wing-tipped shoes packed the place. For an hour a day, they left behind pale walls and the smell of stale paper to plunge into a gaze of girls with light hearts and weighty torsos.

"Of course, because I wanted *you* to see all of the waitresses."

"No! I am not stupid."

"Though you faced the corner, you also had a view behind the counter—where the waitresses bend over to grab the water glasses out of the bottom shelf. You tricked me. I could see your vantage point from the reflection in the mirror behind the counter. You were looking at her bending over!"

Don could not bear the thought of Mr. Marks staring at Rebekka. In Don's mind Rebekka was his—and his alone.

"Hey! Looks like Paul's got a bit of a problem over there." Mr. Marks pointed across the street.

Paul contemplated Thunder. He figured it would be best to lead with his arm. The academy, lacking resources, did not supply the officers with any tools (other than a simple leather leash) to restrain the dogs. He thought about taking off his shirt and wrapping his arm with it. But then he decided against the idea. He did not want to have to purchase another one.

With an angel by his side, Paul rolled up his sleeves. Opened the back door of the car. Looked into Thunder's cold red eyes. Then lunged at him with his left arm forward. The dog's demons emerged and gave Paul a bloody fight. The sonic crack of Thunder boomed through the neighborhood. Capricious stopped. Karl stood. And the two engineers froze.

Paul's wife could not watch. She stepped back into the house. The others could only imagine the event as they saw only a cloud of dust rising from the trembling car and they heard only the sound of Thunder thrashing Paul's flesh.

Moments later the Border Patrol officer emerged. His face revealed no expression. No anger. No pain. No fear. He had figured that if he pushed his left arm far enough into the animal's mouth, back behind his fangs, that he could minimize the damage to his arm. His assumptions proved correct. Though quite bloody, the tears to his forearm appeared not to be too deep.

But Thunder had won the first battle. He defiantly remained in the car. Paul wiped sweat from his brow and paced back and forth like a prizefighter between rounds. No alternate strategy came to mind. Frontal assault would again be deployed.

The two brutes began Round Two. The tornado of decibels and dirt rose above the patrol car once again. The audience watched and listened to the rare show. The dust had cleared a bit from the car's windows. Young Karl, sensing imminent danger, instinctively ran across the street toward Capricious. He stood by her side while her father remained frozen next to Mr. Marks. The young boy's now-apparent affection for the girl had not caught the attention of her father.

Partially muffled by Paul's meaty forearm, Thunder's soul still echoed down through the neighborhood. A sad vicious song touched the understanding innocence of Capricious. She felt the dog's pain—for her parents had told her a story of suffering.

* * *

During the 1930s Capricious's grandmother, Brünhilde, had read an editorial opinion in the *Boston Herald* regarding the health benefits of the dry air in Phoenix. A prominent doctor, Dr. Macon Fülle, had returned to Boston from a vacation at a fancy Phoenix resort.

Life in rural Massachusetts during the Depression was not easy. Brünhilde worked on a tobacco farm hanging leaves to dry during the season. Tobacco had been a staple of the region since before Pilgrims cultivated it, back to the time when Native Americans stuffed religious pipes with it.

The farm on which she worked had been in Brünhilde's Polish husband's family for a generation. But her husband, Henio, lost it after a bout with liquor, jaundice, and the Depression. The new owner, Increase Mather (named after a Puritan minister), did what he could to provide work for them. While he pitied the family, he also exploited the situation. Mr. Mather happily traded with Brünhilde other discreet favors.

For her part she secretly enjoyed the hot, humid, sweaty afternoons with Mr. Mather in the shade under the nets while her husband drank licorice-tasting spirits with fun black-skinned woman. Amid the abundant mellow aroma of curing tobacco plants, she liked the dirty feel of the dark, soft, nutrient-rich Massachusetts soil seasoning her bare bottom. And afterward she liked to smoke fresh cigars—perfectly dried and fermented. Tightly rolled. She had taught Mr. Mather how to pick the best leaves through comparative analysis of peculiar tobacco fragrances.

Brünhilde may have found the dense humidity delightful. Her thirteen-year-old daughter, Capricious's mom, did not. Inflicted with asthma and a weak immune system, Trudi struggled to breath most days. Heavy air transported pollen, dust, fungus, fertilizer, and DTD into her lungs. Audible wheezing came out. And so the family's life evolved around clandestine volition and faint pulmonary grief.

Dr. Macon Fülle's editorial inspired Brünhilde to dream of the sweet sound of silent breathing. Brünhilde had spent so many sleepless nights listening to Trudi's respiration baiting her next breath. As most of the tobacco farm's seasonal workers traveled around the country hopping trains, Brünhilde thought that mode of transportation would be the most expedient avenue of escape. At that point she left behind a note to her husband that stated, "I won't write." And another to Mr. Mather that promised, "I will write."

Mother and daughter found their way to the tobacco-loading train station near the market auction house. They soon discovered railroad detectives swarmed the yards to ward off transients and unlawful vagrants. After spending two nights on bug-infested prison cots at the local eighteenth-century, brick-walled, saltbox-shaped courthouse, the pair found a train just outside the train yard, beyond the location where railroad police hunted for train hoppers.

Like bees to honey, a hundred hobos raced the rails, clinging to open boxcars. Neither Brünhilde nor Trudi were tall enough or strong enough to board a moving pine-planked and cast-iron railcar. Only by the kindness of soot-covered hands did the pair get pulled aboard their sojourn to the unknown.

The hard journey west would consume a year of their lives. In the transient tent "jungles" along the route, the two cooked and cleaned clothes in exchange for food. Across the country they encountered the period's turmoil while choking on freight engine coal smoke. Innumerable defeated families, drifting teens, and homeless rail riders filled their experience. They witnessed a bloody knife fight over a pair of filthy shoes in Defiance, Missouri, and a senseless lynching in the Ozarks. On another occasion behind a blinding bright lantern and a cold steel rifle, the devil's silhouette violently forced its vile nature upon young Trudi. Three months later she pushed out a lifeless soul onto a smooth wooden floor moving at seventy miles an hour. Thereafter, only a short time passed before Brünhilde traded half her leg for a wooden peg beneath a cacophony of deafening and rhythmic rail sounds produced by a goliath locomotive. Trudi then loyally sat by her side during months of rehabilitation at a Catholic hospital faithfully operated by the Diocese of Cheyenne, Wyoming.

Trudi would later tell the story to her companions. She would tell of the journey's only happy day—the day she descended riding the Santa Fe from a cool Prescott breeze into the scorching 117-degree valley heat. Though Trudi recounted burning the fingerprints off her fingers as she made the mistake of touching the freight car's hot metal handle, she rejoiced upon their arrival to their destination.

Unfortunately the happiness was short-lived. Phoenix was no health resort, as Dr. Macon Füller had assured. Brünhilde and Trudi ended up in one of the tent cities on the west side of Phoenix. Primarily populated by those inflicted by tuberculosis, the rumor of safe haven cast upon the city an influx of penniless, labored breathers. After having worked in underground mines for years, some had been cast aside by the local extractive copper, gold, and silver mining industries. Others wandered desperately in from as far as the Midwest Dust Bowl states of Iowa, Kansas, and Missouri. Regardless of their origination, all shared the common affliction of being poor and unhealthy. They also shared the common existence of living under dusty cotton woven tarps beset with exotic disease-ridden rats and mosquitoes.

Community health officials did what they could to provide them with health care. But the resources ultimately proved too scarce to serve the needs of the vast "Lunger" population, which left a legacy of asthma in the Arizona gene pool. In this environment Capricious's grandmother and mother struggled for years.

Ultimately, Brünhilde exploited the curiosity attracted by her peg leg and found employment at a popular dude ranch just outside of Phoenix. She spent the rest of her days permitting onlookers to watch a sharpshooter blow to pieces her peg leg from an impressive distance.

Trudi, during her late teen years, ran off with a short bull rider from Nebraska, who bragged about his large shiny belt buckle, but who wore tiny ropers. Then she tagged along with another who broke his back on a two-thousand-pound Gelbray crowd-pleaser named Aristophanes.

Twenty-some years later during the 1960s, while back in Phoenix, Trudi gave birth to Capricious. She gave her heavy infant in fine fettle to a Mormon couple named Don and Bethany Harmony.

Though for years they had preached preparedness for the Second Coming, the two broke free from the despotism of the Church not too soon after adopting Capricious. Together they explored freethinking and psychedelic music. Absent any guilt, Don indulged his girl study and farmed sticky aromatic marijuana buds in Goodyear until he completed engineering school. He later landed a job in the defense industry calculating collateral damage death rates.

* * *

Paul the patrol officer scratched his head. Round two had finished. Thunder stared through the window at Paul, growling obstinately. Paul came closer to the realization that his dream of becoming a K-9 officer was in serious jeopardy. He accepted defeat. Walked into his home with his head down and his arm bleeding. He called his supervisor.

As Paul waited outside for the supervisor to arrive, the crowd debated a solution.

"They're gonna have to shoot it!" said Mr. Marks.

"Nah, I'm sure they run into this kind of thing all the time," said Don Harmony.

"Yea. And they shoot it!"

Within forty-five minutes an official car of similar appearance as Paul's, having the words "K-9 Supervisor" inscribed along both front-side panels, parked in front of Paul's home. Two tall, thin, serious-looking men in their late forties stepped out of the car and confronted Paul. All three huddled together and murmured tactical two- and sometimes three-syllable monotones. From the trunk of the supervisor's car, they produced a long metal stick with a noose at one end. With great fury and fight, the supervisor negotiated the rope around the dog's head. It took all three men to extract Thunder from his position and muzzle him. For the next hour, Paul sat on Thunder, forcing his three hundred pounds upon the dog. Paul shouted commands again and again. He held Thunder's snout into the ground until the dog finally submitted to Paul.

Paul saved his job.

RAIN

MAY 2004

The First Ladies of Rancho Opulente and the colonel deliberated over the prospect of two pet turtles mating solely for entertainment purposes.

"May I be excused to the ladies room?" C.J. had no interest in turtles. She was thinking about Karl.

"Use the upstairs restroom in the master bedroom over on the right. The movers have been using the ones down here. I think one of them told me the driver has dysentery." Caroline pointed to the ceiling.

As C.J. exited the room, the chatter from the kitchen moved outside to the pool patio. Silence followed her up the grand stairs until the rumbling from one of the teenager's oversized bedrooms drowned out her own thoughts. She heard young voices competing for attention and imagined a circle of kids first learning the group dynamics of flirting with members of the opposite sex. She remembered her own teen years. She never struggled for attention. All her life, by her physical beauty, her commanding personality, and extraordinary understanding of people, she led every group in which she chose to participate. She remembered watching other kids in the group struggle for access and interaction. Growing up, she never showed mercy to anyone. Anyone in her path soon became aware of her patience for neither weakness nor clumsiness.

The wet and coldness from her Bloody Mary glass reminded her that she still held a drink in her hand. She inspected it—the thickness of the vegetable juice and the ground pepper floating across it. She exhaled in disappointment. It did not taste good. Overbearing in every way. She began to feel the alcohol in her head and the spices in her stomach. She felt sad. The fun she had hoped to experience never transpired. And then there was Karl appearing from the past. Then curiosity sparked her awareness of the cathedral ceiling under which she stood.

The grand staircase that led up to the second floor characterized the entire home-so open and spacious. C.J. wondered about the air-conditioning utility bill during the summer months and the heating utility bill during the winter. *The colonel would certainly get an eye-opener, if he even cared at all about the money and energy going to waste.* Level with the second floor on the face of the home, several large picture windows gave the entranceway an even greater sense of openness. The use of natural light would prove architecturally masterful during the months of mild temperatures. However, during the months of sweltering heat, the sunlight would fade all interior materials upon which its ultraviolet rays blazed. C.J. looked out through those vast windows at the then-obstructed view of the Arizona landscape. Only a few months previous, she would have seen a panoramic line of sight that would have captured all of the valley's outlining mountains. The image of huge butterscotch and caramel striped truffle chunks off in the distance would have filled her visual pallet. But unfortunately after only a few months of quick suburban construction across the valley, the colonel's window merely smacked C.J. with the neighbor's stucco eyesore.

She looked down onto the street at the striking moving van parked out front. Karl spoke to the driver. Then it dawned upon her. Karl was speaking to his brother Bram. The terrible memory of the day that Bram's actions changed her life came into her mind; the day that Karl and she rode their bicycles back from the junkyard where they often played together. The day over three decades ago when she learned of...

The Bloody Mary was not agreeing with her stomach. She made it into the restroom and threw up into the toilet. She had only had two sips of alcohol, and they made her ill. Then salty tears from her eyes poured into the flushing bowl as she depressed the handle. That was awful. The past rained on her. She closed the lid and sat on the toilet with her head in her hands. More tears came. Moments later she wiped her eyes with tissue from a newly opened cardboard moving box. A pile of magazines had been dumped next to the box. She rifled through them and found a glossy rose-colored brochure from the Desert Pinnacle of Self Discovery Spa and Boutique. After flipping through the pages, she found a product page describing the Mountains of Fire and Ice Breast Augmentation plastic surgery. Her eyes widened as she read about the saline solution injected with other natural elements, permitting larger, fuller, remote-controlled, temperature-regulated breasts. "With a press of a button, she could surprise her man with Mountains of Fire and Ice."

Meanwhile, outside on the patio, Colonel Gunnar Wiley released Matilda the turtle out into a coliseum of three other onlookers. Matilda inched her way out of the wooden crate. Colonel gave her a little boost by lifting the box at an angle. She slowly slid down and out. The thump of her belly to the Arizona slate-topped patio signaled the colonel to take the box away from the scene. Caroline brought Chester from around the side of the house to meet his new female friend. She placed him two feet from Matilda, and within seconds nature immediately took its course. With great strain Chester pulled himself forward with his four midnight-green stumpy legs. Instinct pointed his compass toward Matilda. Though slow and awkward, he navigated himself with great determination.

"Chester the Molester! Go Chester!" Mrs. Andersen howled and pointed her hands up in the air much like a cheerleader at a college football game.

The crowd cheered and laughed.

Up above, C.J. looked down upon them from the master bedroom window. She opened the window and pressed her face up against the screen. "They have the fish through the window. It's in the trophy room," she said.

The colonel imitated Chester humping his hips back and forth.

"Whooya!" He laughed.

C.J. had no interest in the activities going on below her. She turned into the room and closed the window behind her. The afternoon sun blazed right through its "energy-efficient" double panes and into the room. The air-conditioning did little to ease the rising temperature. Her eyes wandered around the vast master space. The Wileys had brought with them lots of expensive, big, wooden furniture from California. Much of it looked lovingly restored from the eighteen hundreds. She had purchased her modern-style furniture from European galleries and had it all shipped back. But none of it engaged her. She only thought of Karl and Bram. She had finally come to the point in her life when her childhood no longer haunted her everyday. *Why did these two men have to appear out of the blue? Would she be able to forgive Bram? Could she even speak to them?*

Capricious J. Harmony walked out of the colonel's master bedroom and into the hall overlooking the grand staircase leading up to the rail where she stood. After the turtle show, she watched the inebriated group (the colonel, his wife, Mrs. Andersen, and Mrs. Florence) pile through the house toward the trophy room. Then Karl appeared in the front doorway and shined. Their eyes met again, and he smiled at her with welcoming warmth and confidence. With his bright beams, he drew her into him, and she shuddered once again with emotion. This time with her teary eyes she felt comfort, not pain. She smiled too. Karl walked away into the trophy room. C.J. followed.

C.J. walked quietly behind Karl. Amid the smell of fresh paint, new tile, and carpet, she could smell the trail of his cologne. *How did he smell so good after sweating all morning?* With her big zircon eyes, she followed the contours of the *V* in his back and the perfect tone of his gluteus. She watched him move with grace before her. She smiled again, and her neckline too began to blush. It had been so long since she felt this heat—even in the desert.

The entire group then huddled in the trophy room. C.J stepped in behind Karl. Brushed her breasts lightly up against his left arm. She felt his hard flesh against the softness beneath the thin material of her blouse. She walked past him, farther into the room where a raunchy smell preceded the truck driver, Bram, as he entered the room immediately behind her. His stench completely destroyed C.J.'s brief thrill.

"We'd like to mount the fish on the wall," declared Bram.

While the colonel and Bram discussed the hanging strategy, C.J. thought about Karl. The driver's declaration reinforced her realization that Karl would soon be leaving. She would never again set eyes upon him. And again, sadness came. She then resented Karl for the toxic mix of feelings he had inflicted upon her. *At this point in her life, she should have been in control. She always had been. In fact, she decided, she was in control.* C.J. committed to erasing these emotions.

"Perfect!" the colonel agreed to Bram's ideas to hang the swordfish. "Works for me."

While the moving crew began their task, the colonel turned his efforts to rummaging through several boxes strewn about the trophy room.

"I know something else we can put on the wall. It's here somewhere. I remember it's in one of these boxes."

Colonel Wiley ripped open several boxes and strew the contents all over the floor. *Caroline would clean it up. Or the maids would. Somebody. Not him.*

"I know it's here."

C.J. analyzed the content spread around the fourteen-foot fish equating the room's two halves. A veritable collection represented both past and present. Colonel Wiley's father, Major General Wiley, handed down to the colonel the large heads of wild animals he had hunted during his World War II campaign in North Africa. C.J. wondered if the heavy dust emerging from the trophy heads up into the atmosphere originated from half a century ago. She saw an old stained photo of the major general with his five-year-old son, Gunner (the colonel as a child). The boy's innocence clashed with his father's ballistic, determined expression. C.J. would later discover from Caroline that Major General Wiley had asked Senator Gerry Holdwater to promote the major general's son from lowly lieutenant to high-ranking colonel on the day before

Gunnar's retirement. The colonel had earned his title by political favor alone.

Amid the heads of zebra, bison, tiger, and the like, the colonel's small fly-fishing plaques appeared insignificant—names like Beyond the Breakwater Championship, Yakama One Fly Competition and the Wyoming State Fly-fishing Challenge. *Perhaps that swordfish truly promoted the colonel in the eyes of his father's ghost.*

"Found it!"

Once again Colonel Wiley succeeded in shocking the crowd. Above his head he held high a paper poster target filled with bullet holes. A large color photo of Osama Bin Laden served as background to several point rings and ultimately to the target's bull's-eye.

"Caroline and I went target shooting not too long ago. I think this will look just fine hung right up over here!" Colonel Wiley laughed to himself as he spoke.

He nailed the poster up on the wall. Though crooked and not centered, the group marveled at the bullet hole between Bin Laden's eyes. The colonel was a sharp shot. He turned to his guests and smiled proudly.

"They started it. We're gonna end it!"

"Not as long as we are in Iraq. Bin Laden's in Afghanistan. Pakistan by now." C.J. could not resist.

"Al Qaida is in Iraq," the colonel retorted.

"Now they are. But they weren't a year ago when we decided to invade."

"Regardless. Better we fight over there than here. A strong offense is the best defense."

"But at what cost, Colonel? We have done so much damage. The world hates us."

"They don't hate us. They envy us. And besides, the fact that the war is going on over there gives me and you the privilege to sit here and debate it. If it were here, our conversation would be far different."

"I would argue that if we put as much resources into humanitarian efforts worldwide as we do building bombs, we wouldn't have to fear any war at all. And I mean help that is free of religious and political influence."

"Hey, we give billions in aid every year." The colonel grinned.

"But who profits from it? I'll tell you—big US corporations do." C.J. became red with anger. "Look at The World Bank. US corporations and banks are the ones who ultimately benefit from small countries being in debt to large ones. The kind of aid I am talking about has no strings."

"Show me the line in the Constitution that says we are obliged to support the rest of the world. I'll show you the one that says we are supposed to defend ourselves with a military!"

"We were talking about how to prevent wars. I believe if we impose more goodwill than guns, the world will perceive us in a better light. Look at Sweden."

"Look. There is evil in the world. It's a fact. There is good. And there is evil. Christians are good. Muslims are evil." The colonel looked into C.J.'s eyes. Mrs. Florence interjected, "Did you see they swore in a newly elected US Representative into Congress with his hand on a Koran? After everything they did to us on 9/11. Unbelievable. What is this country coming to?"

Meanwhile Karl observed C.J. He watched her cleavage flex as she spoke with passion. While he listened, he made note of every fleshy rhythm as her energy emitted through her voice powerful discourse. He thought about her ideas. He did not consider whether or not he agreed with her. He simply enjoyed her. And he related to her feeling of standing alone in a crowd. The intonation of her sound tickled his ears. She filled him with both her mind and body.

When their eyes met again, he smiled knowingly. He understood her frustration. Each knew discussing politics and religion with most people to be pointless. Neither had the good fortune to meet anyone who shared his or her individual viewpoints. Whereas before in front of the house, they exchanged emotion, in this moment, they shared silent intellectual isolation.

SURGE

AUGUST 1974

On Karl's first day of fifth grade, his mother buttoned his britches, fastened two loops atop the tongue of each of his shoes, and slicked his blond hair. She assured him that the day promised to be grand.

"Straight and tall," she told him to stand. "For behind us all, we find God's loving hand."

Later that day, while the other kids convened in class, a special teacher tutored young Karl. Recently graduated from State, she called herself a speech therapist knowledgeable of the latest technique. She reached to shake his small hand. He thought her plain but pretty and blushed beneath her brilliant gemstone eyes. She asked him his name, and he said nothing.

"Well, that's OK. We have much of the day."

Karl was happy to stay. Together they bayed at the graffiti-stained wall, producing odd sounds with the holes in their heads. This game they played amid the fruity smell of her priceless perfume. Karl was happy this day. With her soft hands, she touched his cheeks. She touched his jaw.

The woman thought they made plenty of progress. The boy merely moaned, as he looked about the hem of her dress.

According to the schedule, the therapist returned Karl to class. Old Mrs. Miller addressed the small-statured audience seated in wooden cradles that she called desks.

"This is the *Inzit*. And this is the *Outzit*. We *will* have an orderly parade of pupils marching into and out of the cloakroom. We enter the cloakroom through this door, the Inzit, and we exit the cloakroom through the Outzit. We will not have anarchy in this room. Does anybody know what anarchy is?"

Karl knew about anarchy. He read about anarchy in his mother's news magazines. A brilliant young boy, he taught himself to read at only age four. But to verbal communication, none of his ideas ever came.

"Anarchy is without order, without rules. In this classroom we have rules and we have order. Therefore, because my classroom is orderly, we enter the cloakroom through the Inzit and we exit the cloakroom through the Outzit. Understood?"

"Yeeessss, Mrs. Miller," the class chanted.

According to the rumor among the members of the local parent-teacher organization, the school board regarded fifth grade as the least important grade, developmentally. Therefore, fifth grade received the least resources and the poorest teachers. The board regularly relegated to the fifth grade all of the washed-up tenured teachers.

"Well, we have a new member of our orderly classroom. Stand up, young man, and state your name for the benefit of the rest of the class. Introduce yourself." She looked at Karl seated in the back of the room next to Capricious.

He stood. Mrs. Miller knew of Karl's disability and proceeded to demonstrate traditional methods of speech therapy to the new young State graduate still standing in the room.

"What's your name, young man?"

The boy stood silent.

"I can't hear you, young man."

The boy stood silent. He stared at the floor. Mrs. Miller scrunched her eyebrows beneath her silver hair. Inflicted with polio since a young age, she used two walking canes and rusty leg braces to permit labored upright mobility. Like a Dungeness crab, she maneuvered herself around to the front of her heavy oak wooden desk and stood just ahead of the first row of students. She smelled of liniments and halitosis.

"Step forward, boy. Come stand here!"

She pointed to the floor just in front of her position. Karl looked at Capricious, and she returned his white fright. The boy inched forward.

"Any day now. Move along. Come here!"

Eerie silence followed the boy and fell upon the class. He counted the twenty-seven faded off-white vinyl tiles until he reached the final plate marked by Mrs. Miller's awful hate. The young speech therapist stood in horror. Afraid, she said nothing.

"So, what's your name?"

The boy stood silent, looking at the floor.

"Answer me, boy."

She waited for a response. None came.

"Look at me." She placed the arch of her cane handle under the boy's chin and raised his face to meet hers.

"Your name is Karl. Isn't it?"

The boy nodded.

"Say it. Say 'Karl!'"

He lost his peripheral vision to a dark cold surge of fear. She still held his chin with the cane. On the bottom of his chin, he could feel her disgusting palm grease on the handle of the cane. Her vile breath suffocated him. He felt dizzy.

"K-K-K. K-K-K. K-K-K." He could hear the name *Karl* in his head, just not in his stuttering voice.

"What in tarnation is that? Spit it out, boy."

Tap. Tap. Tap. She tapped the cane's handle under his chin.

"K-K-K. K-K-K. K-K-K." Again, he heard *Karl* in his head.

"Stop. Stop. No more," the therapist pleaded.

Mrs. Miller turned to the therapist and pointed the rubber tip of her cane toward the therapist's chest.

"You stay out of this!"

"K-K-K. K-K-K. K-K-K."

"How about Hoogeveen? Can you say Hoogeveen?"

"H-H-Hooo. H-H-Hooo. H-H-Hooo."

"Unbelievable. This is anarchy, Karl. There will be no anarchy in this room. You hear me, Karl?"

Mrs. Miller moved two steps to her left.

"Go over there and place both of your hands on my desk."

Karl walked forward into a gauntlet never tame. Facing the chalkboard with his back against the rest of the class, he placed his hands on the desk.

"Again. What's your name?"

"K-K-K. K-K-K. K-K-K."

Whap! Whap! Whap! Mrs. Miller struck Karl's behind with her cane. *Whap! Whap! Whap!*

The boy cried. Hot salty tears rolled down his red swollen face.

"What's your name?"

The boy remained silent.

Whap! Whap! Whap! Then the boy wet his pants, and shame mistakenly forced upon him all of this world's blame.

"Well! I never."

Mrs. Miller turned to the speech therapist.

"Take him to the principal's office. Get him out of here. And tell the janitor to come mop up this mess!"

Upon their exit, Mrs. Miller turned to the class.

"Well. Let's see. I believe it's time for our reading lesson today. Would anyone like to stand and read aloud for the rest of the class?"

While the rest of the class remained in shock, stuck-up Sally Turner raised her hand and smirked.

"Excellent, young lady. Please turn to the first lesson in your reader and begin."

Like a bird from heaven, Sally orated each phrase, each line, each word with perfect pronunciation and song like intonation. She filled Mrs. Miller's heart with gratification. Sally exemplified everything Mrs. Miller's perfect world demanded. The young girl restored order to the class once again. Mrs. Miller grinned. Her horse-like dentures poked through her wrinkled but proper-lady lacquered lips.

"Outstanding. Why don't we continue the section by having another fine student read aloud for the class."

Mrs. Miller looked at a young girl seated in the back of the room. Capricious had caught Mrs. Miller's attention fumbling through her medley of belongings. She had lost her emerald charm bracelet that her older sister, Lucy, had given to her on her tenth birthday.

"What's your name?"

"Capricious Harmony."

"Please stand up and read section two."

Immediately Capricious stood. Mrs. Miller recognized the girl's gift of good looks. She envied the little girl. Wondered what her life would have been like with such a blessing.

"Aaaaa doooog naaaammmed..." Capricious read very slowly, then stopped.

"Continue," Mrs. Miller commanded.

"Ummmm." Capricious paused.

"Go on."

"Ummmm."

"Read the dog's name, please!"

"Ummmm. Rrr. Rrr. Rrr."

"Rover! The dog's name is Rover. Continue!"

"A dog named Rover rrrraaannn up the hill. Hhhheeee..." Capricious paused.

"Read the next word, please."

"Ummmm. Ummmm."

"March forward, young lady. Come here. Stand in front of me." Mrs. Miller pointed to the same tile upon which Karl had just stood.

Capricious walked into the same gauntlet as Karl. She stood before Mrs. Miller.

"Spell the word aloud, please."

"C-H-A-S-E-D." She saw the letters, but the word just did not register in her developing mind.

"What is the *C-H* sound?" Mrs. Miller towered over Capricious.

The girl looked up at Mrs. Miller and said, "Ch."

"That's right. Very good. Ch. Is the *A* sound a long or short *A*?"

"Ummmm."

"Is the *A* sound a long or short *A*?" Mrs. Miller's impatience grew.

"Ummmm."

"Is the A sound a long or short A?"

"Ummmm." Capricious looked at the tile.

"What's the rule?"

"Ummmm."

"There is an *E* at the end of the root word. What's the rule?"

"Ummmm."

Mrs. Miller moved to her left.

"Put your hands on my desk."

Capricious obeyed. She tried in vain to retain her young dignity. She placed her hands on the desk just as Karl had done in preparation for corporal punishment.

"There is an *E* at the end of the root word. What's the rule?"

Capricious did not reply. Mrs. Miller raised the cane. The young girl turned in a flash. With her surge of courage, she grabbed the cane upon its descent toward her person. She blocked its strike. Mrs. Miller attempted to pull the cane from the girl. But the girl's grip was too strong. In shock Mrs. Miller's face turned devil's red. Again she pulled at the cane to gain possession. Mrs. Miller lost her footing and fell back onto the floor. Her leg braces clinked and clanked into knots. The fall confined Mrs. Miller to the floor.

"Go to the principal's office!" Mrs. Miller pointed to the classroom door.

Capricious held her head high despite the old lady's cry. The little girl held her own against the wrinkled tyrant. Queen Capricious then left the classroom and took her throne in the principal's waiting room. She sat next to Karl. They waited for Principal Sullen Peabody to finish his closed-door discussion with Billy the Bully. Then Capricious smiled and snickered. With only her wink, she relieved Karl of his embarrassment, elevating him to his voiceless boyhood a little less lonely.

* * *

On the very same day, at a high school not too far away, Capricious's older sister, Lucy, waited in the cafeteria for Billy the Bully's older sister, Christine. Lucy watched four of the biggest varsity football players surround a lone freshman seated at a table attempting to eat his lunch. One of the football players took the freshman's chocolate pudding. To everyone's surprise the freshman stood up and punched the offender straight in the mouth. True anarchy ensued.

"Come on! Let's go! Nobody's watching!" Christine grabbed Lucy's arm.

Both teens wore self-woven macramé headbands, rose-colored glasses, tie-dyed shirts and bell-bottoms. They ran through the girls' sweat-smelling locker room located next to the wooden gymnasium and out the school's dark steel back door.

Across the unpaved school service road they ran, hungering for a taste of freedom. The square school's dark-red bricks soon dropped into the small green hill behind them. The two fantasized about an off-campus lunch with Karl's older brother, Bram.

Lucy had never before been to "the Rock." Other students had informed her of its sinful inspiration, and of the tawdry fate that awaited her atop that burning desert slate. Only with Christine had Lucy dared to share her "older man" date.

Into the woods they traveled. Up a hidden small path they followed. A clearing in the trees revealed a car-sized boulder spray-painted with poetic exploits. Tall, thin, and muscular-cut Bram lay across the top of the Rock. He appeared to Christine as an edible male model—one she had seen in one of the newly published skin magazine layouts. Both Lucy and Christine tickled with excitement.

"Hello, ladies." Bram grinned.

He wore only his cutoff jeans. His long blond hair draped over his copper shoulders. He stood and greeted each with a peck and a warm embrace. The girls' heads spun and spun. He gave each many looks as they consumed a lunch including heisted champagne and ripe strawberries lovingly contributed by Lucy. Then he introduced them to a bubbling, exotic, glass water pipe, funny-smelling marijuana, and a whole new habit of dizzy fun. Finally fulfilling both of the girls' father's fears, under the shaded desert sun on the infamous hot Rock, Bram composed a miraculous three-part composition entitled *Ménage à Trios Dénudé.* Then Bram carved a heart shape into the bark of an old mesquite next to the Rock. Into it he inscribed, "Bram Loves Lucy and Christine." The three became forever inseparable.

HAIL

A few months after Thunder, the Border Patrol canine, introduced himself to the neighborhood, Capricious once again rode her pretty bike in circles and figure eights. She had always enjoyed being different, even at age ten. Her bike was different. Her clothes were different. All very tasteful, of course. But to some small extent, her combinations proved slightly extravagant. She expressed her confidence through her style and her recalcitrant pride.

Capricious adhered to an authoritarian instinct. Therefore, as Karl watched her from within his garage, sitting on his Blue Flame bicycle, she refused to acknowledge him like other girls did. Within their blossoming human intuitions, Karl would look to her and not the reverse. She required it that way.

Voiceless Karl stood up on the bike's pedals and rode down the driveway toward Capricious. She knew he approached but pretended not to notice. In a brief moment, Karl parked himself in the middle of the street just in her path. He proudly hung his leg over the midnight-blue bike's black banana seat. Capricious eyed the yellow, orange, and red flames that decorated its chain guard. She stopped and looked at Karl's radiant sapphire eyes.

"Hi," she said.

"H-H-H-Hi," he replied.

"So you do talk?"

"N-N-N-Not much."

"I think you can say your name." Capricious smiled coyly.

Karl felt immensely comfortable in her presence. He leaned forward. Placed his nose above her left ear. Breathed in her clean scent and whispered, "Karl Hoogeveen." The he stepped back and shouted to the world, "Karl Hoogeveen!" The young boy could not believe his ears. He said his name for the very first time.

"I knew you could do it." Capricious jumped up and down.

"Y-Y-Y-You wanna go kill some frogs with me?" Karl asked confidently.

"There aren't any frogs around here, silly."

"Sure there are. Over at Farmers Pond."

Farmer Barlow had sold a corner of his cotton acreage to a developer. Capricious and Karl stood upon that plot in their new neighborhood. Just across a field of cotton and past the dairy farm, Farmer Barlow and Farmer

McNealy shared rights to a pond and the natural underground wells and man-made aqueducts that fed it.

"You afraid to g-g-g-go?" Karl poked.

"No."

"Maybe your m-m-m-mom won't let you go."

"I can go. I just need to tell her that I am going."

"So you'll go."

"OK."

Capricious ran into her house. Capricious's mom, Bethany, wearing a Citrine Jersey wrap, and her Aunt Abish sat at the kitchen table. Bethany's mom named her older sister Abish after one of the six women mentioned in the Book of Mormon. The family considered the name and the questions it attracted a great missionary opportunity. By explaining the name's origin, they could proceed to an in-depth discussion of the Book Of Mormon and the benefits of joining the church.

Underneath her conservative white blouse and azurite blue skirt, Abish wore her white temple undergarments manufactured by the Zion's Clothing Mill in Utah. The Church of Latter-day Saints endowed her to wear them, and she believed they protected her against temptation and evil. Bethany, in contrast, chose not to wear any undergarments at all. She liked the spark of a hot desert breeze and tickle of a free bounce when she walked.

Abish admired the new brand-name, color-coordinated, avocado appliances that Don and Bethany Harmony had purchased. The sleek contemporary designs offered conveniences for the day's modern lifestyle. The self-cleaning double-range oven featured versatile electronic cooking that could simultaneously bake and brown food. The two-door upright refrigerator included the new water and ice dispenser on the front door. Since Bethany and Don had left the church, Abish assumed that they had not been using their blessings to build the kingdom of God. She supposed that they reveled in selfish materialism. In reality the Harmonys donated both time and money to worthy community charities.

"Remember, Bethany, wealth and perishables 'are liable to decay the minds of saints.'" Abish recounted President Brigham Young's warning.

Bethany sighed. Her wheels spun. She could bite her lip no longer. "You know what I think?" she said.

"Bethany, I never know what you think!" Abish turned her head away from her and smirked.

"I think all men are pigs."

"What does that have to do with Brigham Young?"

It's all a farce. Men are motivated by one objective. Everybody knows it-each hog driven by a single cog. Brigham Young and Joseph Smith are no exception!"

Her sister gasped. "You're going to hell for saying such blasphemy. I can't believe you just said that. Take it back! Pray for forgiveness!"

"Do you truly think polygamy is a revelation from God given to a prophet?"

Abish sat motionless.

"I bet you anything that Joseph Smith's wife caught 'em cheating. And like any man caught with his pants down, he comes up with some wild story-a revelation-that God commands men to have multiple wives. So he rewrites the New Testament to get out of hot water. It goes to my point that a man will say and do anything to cheat and get away with it!"

Abish shook her head. "You're going to hell!"

Bethany did not pay attention to her sister. Instead, she peered over Abish's shoulder and watched her contemporary color-technology TV in the corner of the family room. The news of Caesar Chavez's hunger strike at the local United Farm Workers headquarters had been making Phoenix headlines. She sympathized with the UFW. The Arizona Legislature had recently passed House Bill 2134 outlawing collective bargaining, produce boycotts, and strikes during harvest season. She had stopped purchasing grapes and lettuce in support of the UFW.

After Capricious popped into the house to ask her mom's permission to go to Farmers Pond, Bethany replied, "Don't be too long, sweetie!"

As Capricious returned outside, Karl hopped like a frog around her bicycle in preparation for the ritualistic slaughter about to take place. She smiled. Never before had she contemplated taking a life. Something basic stirred inside her. Karl had touched her.

The boy had earned the privilege to ride ahead of her. He took the lead. For the first time, she felt comfortable following. She liked the motor sound of his bike. He had taken a wooden clothespin from his mom's laundry room and used it to clip a baseball card to the front fork. As he pedaled and the wheel spun, the card vibrated across the moving spokes. To them it sounded like an American-made muscle car.

Capricious followed him and his sound. She could smell him. He smelled clean. His mom used expensive detergent. Pressed his clothes with love. He wore jean cutoffs and a bright, thick, white T-shirt. She noticed. She watched the dusty wind part his blond hair as he bounced up and down on the bicycle. She blindly followed, uncharacteristically not looking for oncoming cars. She found a new level of comfort riding second, not caring for

what lay ahead or behind. To the end of the neighborhood
they came.

"Let's stop here first," Karl ordered Capricious.

She stopped. Both were red-faced and sweaty from
the desert heat and the ride.

"Let's get some bubble gum and grape soda," he said.

Karl led her around to the back of the El Toro Corner
Convenience Store. Behind a ten-foot-high chain-link fence
lay stacks and stacks of empty soda bottle cases that had
been returned to the store for recycling, in exchange for the
redemption price of a nickel per bottle. Skillfully Karl
scaled the fence and handed down to Capricious two
cardboard six-packs of empty bottles. Fearing the
consequences of being an accomplice to grand theft, she
looked around for witnesses to the crime as she received the
bottles from him. She remembered the group of teenagers
loitering in front of the store. *Had they seen them? Would
they wonder where the two had suddenly come up with
twelve bottles for return?*

"Let's go!"

Karl led Capricious back around to the front of the
store. Each carried a carton of bottles. Karl recognized Billy
the Bully and his mean cohorts. He knew they waited
outside the store, asking older store patrons of legal age to
help them buy cigarettes. They typically found sympathetic

souls in the form of Mexican farmhands stopping in to the store to pick up twenty-four-ounce cans of malt liquor Dust Cutters and cartons of *Caballero* Killer cigarettes.

A family of sixteen young attractive Latina sisters operated the store. Mr. Parks, the Korean owner, knew he could charge a premium price for his goods, knowing the farmhands would pay any price he set for only the chance to see the sisters behind the counter. Mr. Parks' business model was quite similar to Harry's Diner just down the road.

As Karl and Capricious entered the store, Billy the Bully barked at them. Karl ignored his sound and proceeded into the store. In Mr. Parks' absence, Karl understood the sisters transacted various goods "under the counter." His older brother Bram had informed him of the black-market economy sustained at the store. Benefitting from Lyndon Johnson's Great Society, several of the young second-generation Mexican American mothers sold food stamp baby formula on consignment through the store.

Karl ignored the nature of such discourse occurring at the counter and led Capricious to the candy shelves and then to the refrigerator, where each selected a cold bottle of grape soda. After redeeming the pilfered bottles' return value and purchasing their treats, the two kids proceeded outside back to their bikes. Billy the Bully was engaged in a discussion with a kind stranger. With their goodies in Capricious's white bike basket, the two made way without incident. Capricious's adrenaline pumped with thrill and relief.

Afterward they hid their bicycles under Farmer Barlow's cotton plants a few rows in from the road. The terrain forced them on foot for the remainder of the trip. Karl opened the soda bottles by popping each on the edge of his bike pedal. As they sucked down sugary grape soda and chewed on gobs of sour apple bubble bum, they walked through a field of dead cotton infected with southwestern cotton rust disease.

The heat carried the dense smell of the neighboring dairy cow manure through the cotton fields. The closer they came to the diary farm, the more unbearable became the stench.

"Don't worry, the pond is upwind from the cows," Karl said, turning to Capricious. "It doesn't smell there."

Trudging through the freshly irrigated muddy field (As the farmhands were striking, Farmer Barlow had not yet been informed by the staff that the cotton had died.), Capricious momentarily contemplated her soiled tennis shoes. Never before during her young life had anything of hers been so dirty. The adventure was worth it. Handsome, charming Karl was worth it. She gleamed with unfettered credulous joy.

"Stinky moo cows!" Karl pinched his nose and smiled. "Look!" He pointed beyond the dead cotton to the herd.

A hundred hot dairy cows stood together chewing cud beneath a shiny aluminum cover. The farmhands had built a makeshift water mister just above the cows under the shelter. Several rusty old fans slowly turned, blowing piped-in water drips over the cows to create a mist that absorbed desert heat upon the water's evaporation.

Escaping the sun, three striking farm workers sat crouched down at the end of the structure, eating watermelon and spitting seeds. Above them hung a large UFW poster that read, *"Si Se Puede!"* The three, two men from Ecuador and the other from Guadalajara, listened to competing AM radios. The Ecuadorians attempted to listen to *El Copa Libertadores de América.* The Mexican refused to listen to any *futbol* competition that did not involve his homeland team. He rudely blared his AM radio tuned to the thumping brass, wind, and accordion ensemble music proclaimed *La Musica De La Raza.*

Farmer McNealy had not kicked them off the land. He too sympathized with the UFW cause and permitted the workers to strike on his property despite the hardship to his bottom line. Being a kind and humble man, he treated his workers with kindness. He built comfortable housing for them on his land. Sponsored their legal immigration and paid them fair wages. Yet Farmer McNealy and his workers proved to be the exception. Their counterparts who worked as migrant farm workers traveling from state to state, according to the harvest seasons, suffered terrible working conditions. Their plight served as the catalyst for the UFW strikes and boycotts.

Karl and Capricious ran through the cow pen in hopes the men would not see them. All three men whistled and hooted as the kids tore through the yard. Capricious's clothes increasingly attracted more and more mud. A few dark speckles soiled her face and brown hair. Karl's white shirt lost its luster.

On the other side of the cow pen, the two kept running toward Farmers Pond. Its black-green water reflected the sun in a million different directions. Their gum had lost its flavor. Karl spit out his, and Capricious did the same. They both smiled at each other. A wisp of heated breeze tapped at them. Karl led Capricious down the pond's shoreline to his secret bay covered with hundreds of huge flowering Victoria water lilies. With the morning's rising sun, the lilies' buds had opened. With the stench of the dairy farm no longer nearby, Karl and

Capricious could smell the lilies' beautiful fruity scent as they approached. They had found paradise.

Karl held Capricious's hand as the two boarded his shore-docked raft that he had built with stolen housing construction wood. Neither had ever held hands like that before. Both blushed. Both cherished the touch.

Karl used a perfect stick to push the craft away from the shore and into the water lilies. From the stern he propelled the raft with the stick. He examined Capricious sitting at the bow, looking ahead into the future. He watched the gentle motion of the lilies parting around her. During his young life, he had never experienced anything more pleasing. He would remember that moment forever.

Past the Port of Lilies, Karl used his keen sense of latitude and longitude to push the vessel along the shoreline over to Freaky Frog Cove. He made sure not to go beyond the pond floor's shelf. His stick was not long enough to reach the pond bottom beyond the shelf's underwater edge. He had made this voyage many times before, but not with such precious cargo. As captain of the *Goodyear Frogger*, he would ensure the safety of the ship's passenger.

After the euphoria of Karl and his lilies had passed, Capricious noticed red stains on the deck. She assumed these were from previous blood voyages. She postulated the method and tools Karl used for the hunt. By his feet rested an old dirty satchel stenciled with the words USMC LT HOOGEVEEN. *What was inside?*

Their arrival to Freaky Frog Cove would soon satisfy her curiosity. He ran the raft ashore prior to reaching the cove.

"Shhhh. Don't scare the frogs."

Karl grabbed the satchel in one hand and Capricious's forearm in the other. They tiptoed up to the cove. A chorus of throaty frog bass tones filled their paradise. Karl smiled.

"They're *huge!*" Capricious's eyes widened.

"Shhhh."

Karl reached into his bag of goodies and withdrew a metal slingshot that his brother had purchased from an Apache reservation and several dull raw copper ore pellets.

"I got these from the train tracks over there."

The Arizona Copper Company Railroad Engine No. 7, an old Baldwin 2-8-2 built in 1917, pulled copper ore up from the Arizona Copper Company mine located down in Superior near Tucson. The industry's legacy stretched back to the late nineteenth century, during which time Arizona copper mines fueled much of the industrial revolution and the demand for copper wire. Spilling a tiny fraction of its load as it barreled through town, old No. 7 provided him with bullets for his weapon. "Look!" Karl pointed out to the cove.

A moaning bullfrog sat on an Amazon-sized lily. Karl loaded his weapon with a copper bullet. Pulled back the sling. Took aim. Then fired. The slingshot snapped and launched the ammunition. The noise frightened the frogs. Hundreds of them jumped into the water, disturbing the cove's serenity with great ruckus and calamity.

"Look! I got 'em!"

Experience had taught Karl to lead the frog with his pellet. He knew the slingshot's snap would alarm the frog and that the frog would instinctively jump. By shooting the pellet ahead of the frog, he could hit it as it leaped.

Capricious looked out onto the blood-slick-covered water. The bullfrog floated yellow belly up. The realization of the event transcended her earlier enthusiasm. She felt sad. Karl had killed that frog. She began to cry.

Puzzled, Karl did not know how to react. Then he too felt remorseful. Not for the frog. But for Capricious. He took responsibility for making his new treasured love unhappy. *Would she hate him?*

"I'm sorry, Capricious. Come on. Let's go!"

Normally Karl would have floated out on the raft to retrieve his kill. Then on the ship's deck, he would have blown up the frog with the Black Leopard firecrackers he got from the Apache reservation. But none of that enterprising sport would occur on that day. Capricious changed everything.

Instead, he and his teary-eyed first mate boarded the boat and pushed along farther around the pond's edge. They came upon another inlet, where they sought to recover from the severe amplitude of their oscillating emotions. Beneath the shade provided by a large mesquite tree, they collapsed upon a large soft military tarp that Karl had always used to cover and hide his raft while docked at night.

Capricious looked upon her scared person and her soiled garments. Once again her eyes watered.

"What I am gonna do? I am so messy." She sniffled.

"I know. We can wash our clothes and bathe in the pond."

"What?"

"Yes. We'll jump in the pond! The sun will dry our clothes in no time!"

"What do you mean?"

Karl said nothing. Capricious knew what he meant. Her innocent instinct and confidence then guided her. She stood up and removed her blouse and shorts, revealing her youthful undergarments.

"Your turn!"

Karl did the same and then removed his trousers. He stood before her wearing only his bright undershorts. Together they waded in the shallow water, rinsed the day's dirt from their clothes, and began splashing one another with newfound glee. Karl and Capricious jumped up and down, screaming with joy. Their toes squished in the mud. Happy. Happy. Happy.

Then the moment settled into quiet bliss. Capricious looked at Karl. Karl looked at Capricious. They smiled.

"Capricious, I have something to show you."

From his father's Marine Corps satchel, Karl produced a small paperback copy of *The Adventures of Tom Sawyer*, by Mark Twain.

"This is a very famous book," he said. "I'm gonna help you. I know you can read it."

In simple terms that only a brilliant boy could express to an eager-to-learn young girl, Karl explained to Capricious the fundamentals of phonics and linguistics. And for the first time, she understood. Together, slowly, they read aloud until Karl gently reduced his voice to a whisper in the wind. Then Capricious read alone while Karl listened with a broad smile on his pink face. For the remainder of their special childhood bond, Karl would continue to tutor Capricious at the pond.

"I know about the real Blue Flame." She changed the topic of conversation from *Tom Sawyer* to his bicycle's namesake. "It's that jet car. The fastest in the world."

"Wow, you're pretty smart," said Karl.

Capricious's face turned rose. They both smiled and closed their eyes. Emotion and the desert heat nudged both of them gently into a quiet afternoon nap.

A lazy hour passed. Capricious opened her eyes to see a sky the color of her favorite ice-blue Popsicle. As she turned her head to Karl, he had already been looking at his new sky. He had been looking at her. They smiled. Then dressed into their dry, clean clothes.

"Can you keep a secret?" Capricious turned serious.

"Sure."

In that instant a hailstorm of copper ore pellets rained down upon them. One of them hit Karl and left a gash in the side of his belly. He bled slightly. It stained his white T-shirt. Capricious screamed and turned to see Billy the Bully and his crew in the distance, laughing. Earlier they had stolen Karl's weapon and cache while the two kids had diverted into the pond to bathe. The frog hunter had become the hunted, and the horror of the situation came into him like a bolt of lightning striking the earth.

"It's Karl the Stutterer and Capricious the dummy."

Billy and the followers surrounded them. They howled, "C-C-C-Come on, K-K-K-Karl. Say somethin', stupid!"

After the incident in Mrs. Miller's classroom, everyone knew he had a severe stutter. Outside of his immediate family, Capricious was the first to ever hear him speak.

"I got a better idea. How about if Capricious reads aloud for us."

The bullies knew she had a slight reading disability; that she was in the special reading program at school; that neither Karl would speak nor Capricious would answer their question. Capricious exploded. She jumped up and lunged at Billy, pushing him back onto his heels. In the commotion Karl grabbed his new love by the arm and ran with her to the safety of the raft. The gang of bullies chased them. Fired copper hail at them. And upon Karl's launch of the raft away from the shore, they took his perfect raft push stick from his grasp. They roared with laughter as Karl and Capricious floated out into the pond beyond the underwater bottom shelf. They watched the two drift out into deep water. Karl turned to Capricious and said, "I can't swim."

While Karl and Capricious drifted into deep water, Billy the Bully and his friends grew restless. The cruel fun had ended. They abandoned the pond in favor of smoking cigarettes behind one of the aluminum dairy cow barns.

Out on the raft, the two assessed their predicament.

"Are you scared?" Capricious asked.

Karl thought about it. "No. I just can't swim. Dunno what we're gonna do, is all."

"Well, I'm on the junior swim team," Capricious assured Karl.

"So you're gonna leave me here and swim all the way to the shore over there? It's kinda far, don't you think?"

"I can make it."

Capricious had never swum more than fifty meters. And even then her laps were in closely guarded pools never far from safety. Looking from the raft toward the distant shore, her overconfidence exceeded her preadolescent judgment. She only saw *terra firma* and only felt the desire to be home again.

"It's too far, Capricious. I have a better idea. We can both hang onto the raft and kick with our feet to push it."

"What if you slip? You'll drown," Capricious warned.

"I won't slip."

Both of them were quite dehydrated from being in the sun all day. And both were weak, sweaty, and red-skinned. In quick time their condition under the Arizona desert blaze hastened a desperate attempt. Capricious insisted that she enter the water and that Karl remain topside. In the water she held on to the *Frogger's* edge. Karl spared Capricious his knowledge of the snake-infested waters, as he had seen snakes on previous occasions at the pond. He opted instead to keep watch for slithering ripples as she paddled against the raft's stern edge.

Swoosh. Swoosh. Swoosh. Swoosh. She paddled with all of her tiny might. She pushed the heavy waterlogged *Frogger* against the critical oncoming current. Pond waves splashed up and over the raft's blunt bow. Capricious's legs burned. Foul-tasting water filled her mouth. But persistence served as her compass.

She stopped to rest. With her head poking out of the pond's surface, exhausted, she looked up at Karl. He gave her a deep look of assurance. And then she kept paddling for the thirty-minute duration until they reached the shore.

"Capricious! You did it!"

Drained of all her physical, emotional, and mental capacity, Capricious replied, "Maybe next time we'll just play house." Then she thought about it some more and said, "Nahhh. This was the greatest day ever!" They smiled.

CALM

T he morning after the colonel's move, the rising sun pierced through an opening in the wooden blinds and heated Karl Hoogeveen's heavy eyelids. It woke him from deep slumber. His watery eyes had glued themselves shut through the night. Karl barely had the strength to open his eyes to greet the day. Then every sore muscle in his body reminded him of the previous day's activity. His stiff bones ached.

Finally able to peek through one eye, he noticed the maple slats in the blind beginning to fade and bow from direct exposure to desert light. He had paid four hundred dollars for the window cover. He had been living in one of the first homes built in Rancho Opulente; it had only been one full summer, and the second was only beginning. He had shipped the blinds all the way from Vermont, and the sunlight had already begun wearing them down.

He exhaled with exhaustion and began a slow routine to move his limbs. First his tanned left hand and feet. Then he wiggled his muscular legs. He could feel the blond hair on his legs tickle the clean and pressed bright white bedsheets. He moaned in pain.

"When are you going to stop?" scolded a tiny five-foot-nothing brunette woman laying next to him. She wore one of his large cotton T-shirts. Her otherwise sweet voice salted his deep wounds.

"You're forty-two years old. You're a family man. You have to think of your children. And me. What if you had been injured? Or had a heart attack? There is no reason for you to be moving furniture!"

"He's my brother. He needed my help. He had dysentery. He couldn't do any of the moving himself." Even speaking pained Karl.

"You could have hired someone in your place."

"Good people are hard to find on short notice. And besides, I like the exercise. I hadn't worked out in four days."

"You call that exercise? That's the last time. No more."

"OK. No more," Karl conceded.

While his younger wife, Nineveh, fluttered out of the king-sized bed and ran downstairs and out to the backyard, Karl felt the pain of his Achilles tendons as he stepped out of bed. He limped to the window and looked through the sun-weathered blinds. Karl watched his wife watering backyard plants. Her parents had named her after the Old Testament city depicted in "Jonah and the Whale." The neighbor woman sat under a queen palm in the shade next to Nineveh. Karl knew the neighbor sang about her troubles. Most people found comfort being in Nineveh's nonthreatening presence. Karl loved that unique rare quality in her. He observed with pride as Nineveh gave the neighbor a handful of fresh dove eggs that Nineveh harvested from her birdcages located around the side of the house. As a child growing up in a dirt-poor Mexican village, she learned an old wives remedy. She believed dove eggs controlled epileptic seizures. The neighbor's kid had just been diagnosed.

Karl also loved his wife's gift of gardening. He continued to look out the window at his wife tending to her plants. She had planted both indigenous and other varieties throughout the entire yard (and in every room indoors). Each and every day she touched each plant. She gave such life to the home. Even out there in the desert, each of her plants rewarded her with dark green color, bright flowers, and thick rich leaves. While her neighbors stood in line at the local nursery returning dead plants under warranty, Nineveh lavished in blooming beauty. Karl loved her deeply.

Nineveh knew Karl watched her from above. She could feel him. Her beauty never tired or bored him. *She was really something.* Karl smiled when she looked up at him during her return indoors.

Then Karl slipped away into his memories. He thought of Capricious and of the day long ago that she erased his stutter and gave his voice meaningful sound. She freed him of his silent isolation from the world and of the wretched feeling of not being able to communicate with other human beings. While it took formal speech therapy over a long period of time for Karl to overcome completely his stuttering disability, Capricious gave him the initial confidence and patience to verbalize his thoughts.

Capricious had grown up into such a beautiful C.J.—harmonious in every way. He thought about her perfect contours. About her fleshy motions gyrating in rhythm to her tenacious tones as she confronted the colonel in the trophy room. In Karl's mind he replayed again and again the recent sight and glory of his childhood love as a woman. Adrenaline and testosterone flowed through him, tuning his desire.

As his subconscious returned him to his present day, he turned to see the armoire and the rest of the master bedroom set. At the time when Karl and Nineveh as newlyweds purchased the set, he could not afford the complete package with all of the pieces included. He spent several thousand dollars on the dark wood bed, the two nightstands, and the dresser. For years Nineveh lacked a sense of being whole until Karl completed the set by giving her the armoire for their tenth wedding anniversary. On that day he witnessed her rare smile as she checked off the missing armoire from her list of wants.

As a measure of control, Nineveh rarely gave Karl the satisfaction that he had succeeded in pleasing her. She consciously kept him working for her approval. Karl recognized her motive. He also realized that ultimately he controlled the relationship. He permitted her to win small day-to-day battles while he made the bigger decisions. According to this dynamic, each maintained a sense of power and balance within the relationship.

Karl walked down to the first floor. At the bottom of the stairs, he looked over at the bubbling and whirling two-thousand-gallon fish tank located in the converted formal living room. Nineveh, appalled that a formal living room hosted a dark pool of ugly sturgeon and mean king crab, rarely stepped her foot into the space. Karl, quite the opposite, spent a fair amount of time in that room, dreaming while he looked into the tank at its contents. He fantasized about farm-raised sturgeon producing fancy caviar and of breeding and harvesting genetically engineered king crab. Both species proved next to impossible to keep outside their natural habitat. He had been corresponding with university professors living in Russia and in Alaska to overcome the challenges of domesticating these forms of life. The sturgeon refused to give him eggs, and the king crab still needed at least four more tumultuous years in captivity before maturing into commercial-sized adults. The professors warned him not to spend too much money on the endeavors. Though the odds were against him, Karl held onto the vision of the Arizona King Crab and Caviar Company. While he commanded control of his personal relationships, he still reached for control of a business.

A moment later his two children, Sven and Karla, began arguing somewhere in the house. He could hear their high-pitched screeches penetrating the walls. The sturgeon and crab took cover in fear.

"Hey! Cut it out!" Karl roared. "Jesus." He whispered and shook his head.

His pace quickened as he hobbled into the kitchen. The pain from the previous day's activity still inflicted its bite. Nineveh greeted him with a sarcastic smirk, shaking her head as she observed him limp. The kids ran in circles around him and through the kitchen. Sven, age twelve, chased Karla, age eight.

"Sven's been eating in his room again. I found a full cup of milk and cookie crumbs all over the floor. He left a ring on the wooden dresser. I can't get it off! *Cuantos veses que se dije?*" She slipped into Spanish and pointed a wooden spoon at Karl.

"Mom didn't even let me explain," said Sven, defending himself. "All she did was come into my room and start screaming at me. If she would listen! It was Karla!"

"I didn't do it! It was Sven."

"How many times have I asked you, Karl, to talk to him? He never listens. I am sick of it," Nineveh injected.

"Daddy! Daddy! Daddy! It was Sven."

"Bull!" Sven grabbed Karla.

"Hey! Don't touch your sister." Karl gently yanked Sven. "Sven, look me in the eye and tell me if you left that cup and crumbs in your room."

"You don't need to ask him anything. I am telling you he left that stuff in there. Why are you asking him? I am telling you the story." Nineveh grasped for control.

"Dad! See? Mom never listens to me."

"That's because you never listen to me." Nineveh pointed the spoon at Sven.

"Is it possible for me to have a discussion with my son without you interrupting? I am talking to Sven. Please do not interrupt me." Karl took control.

"Daddy. Daddy. Daddy. Can I have a chocolate donut for breakfast?" Karla looked up at him with her cute blue eyes.

"Uh." Karl thought about her diet for the last few days. "I dunno. Ask your mother." He turned to Nineveh. "Has she been eating well lately?"

"Yes. Yes. Yes, Daddy. I had fruit and vegetables and chicken and rice and only one candy yesterday."

"It's OK with me if it's OK with your mother," Karl said and turned to the kitchen cabinet and grabbed his favorite off-white coffee cup. "How's the coffee this morning?" he asked as he turned to Nineveh. Sven's offense had been forgotten. The kids grabbed donuts and ran out of the room.

"Hey! Eat in the kitchen, please. Get back here!" Karl roared again.

Sven returned to the kitchen.

"I'm not going to church today," announced Sven.

Nineveh looked at Karl with red boiling eyes. Karl looked at Sven with the same and pounded his fist on the table.

"You're going to church!"

"Are you going?" Sven asked his father.

"No." Karl had moved away from God.

"That's not fair," Sven proclaimed.

"Life's not fair," Karl replied.

"Daddy. Don't you want to be with me wearing the new orange sherbet dress you bought me?" Karla looked again at her father with her pretty blue eyes.

"Uh...Nah. I don't wanna go."

"Please, Daddy."

"It's not fair that we have to go and you don't," said Sven. "Come on! You never go to church," he said, demanding justice.

"Please, Daddy."

"Uh." Karl looked at Karla and sighed. "OK. Keep calm. I'll go just this once." He melted.

"You're not wearing that dress." Nineveh turned to Karl. "She wore it to church three weeks ago. It's too soon. I don't want people to see her in the same outfit twice. Wear the new white one!"

"Noooooo! I want to wear sherbert dress. And besides...Mommy wore her white blouse two times. I saw her. Two times! It's not fair."

Karl rolled his eyes, picked up his coffee cup, and left the kitchen. Nineveh followed him and met him in the man cave in which the sturgeon and crab swam with stoic indifference. Karl sat behind a large wooden desk and slurped on his java. It burned as it slid down the back of his throat into his stomach. He liked the feeling of burning coffee inside his belly.

"Honey, look! I found this great advertisement for a new leather chair." Nineveh smiled at Karl.

Immediately, Karl began thinking about this month's financial position. He had left a high-paying job to earn sweat equity in his current business venture, a rainbow trout fish farm and artificial river technology company. He served as the company's chief technology and biological engineer. His investment of time in the firm represented only a small fraction of the business. Several other partners and a board of directors held controlling interest of the company.

For now, the Hoogeveens lived check to check, month to month. They lived on hope and on hard work. Karl believed in the potential of the business. The company had its first installation—the Rainbow Rapids located right in his own community, Rancho Opulente. In the booming Phoenix economy, he had nothing to fear. Several new installations were in the pipeline.

While Nineveh spoke about purchases for the home, Karl looked at her warmly and deeply. Every so often he would sprinkle in a nod and a murmur. Simultaneously in his mind, he went through the list of current bills he faced. The family had the air-conditioning repair bill, his speeding ticket, Sven's soccer club dues, Karla's tumbling class tuition, Nineveh's college tuition, Sven's emergency room bill for his sprained ankle, his brother Bram's bail after a bar fight incident, their anniversary was coming up, the summer vacation…The list seemed endless to him.

"And I know twelve hundred is a bit steep, but it's half off, and we can pay it off over a year. *No te precupas!*" Nineveh smiled and rubbed his shoulders.

Actually, she was great with money. Knowing each store's prices, she planned with great care every trip to the market. Nineveh approached shopping as an expression of love for her family. Every dollar she saved reflected her passion and appreciation for her family. And her husband understood.

Karl knew her peppering him with purchase requests provided her with a topic of conversation and a means to interact with him. In response to Nineveh rubbing his shoulders, Karl flexed his big upper-body muscles and slurped his coffee with a wink and a smile.

"We can think about it. I think it would be a great addition to the house."

After the moment passed, Nineveh left the room. Karl's wife was happy. Everything was calm, like the calm before a great storm. Upon her exit, he immediately began scribbling a clandestine note addressed to C.J.

Two Twisters

Billy the Bully stared at Principal Sullen Peabody sitting across from him behind a large but cheap wooden desk. Hanging on the wall above Principal Peabody's head, a worn wooden paddle captured Billy's interest-drawing his attention away from the principal's drowsy dialect. Bushy-haired Billy pointed his nose toward Mr. Peabody, but his eyes wandered upward. The white oak paddle looked deceivingly soft. Perfectly rounded edges and smoothly sanded surfaces served as evidence of the fine craftsmanship and love applied during its fabrication by the paddle's artisan. Billy concluded that it must have been constructed over at the high school's woodworking shop. Burned into the paddle's face was the word *Ernesto*.

"Our school, along with all the other schools in the district, has rules and expectations. We've discussed the importance of following these rules many times, Billy. We have also discussed the consequences of not following these rules. Needless to say, your behavior is not very good. You are constantly off task-talking or walking around the room during instructional time, not reading during the assigned times, not lining up quietly when the class is led down to lunch, and most importantly, it appears that you have aggression issues. You don't seem to socialize well with the other students. Given that your grades are pretty good, straight Bs, I honestly don't understand. I've discussed your situation with the school counselors. We are not quite sure what to do, Billy. Can you help me out?"

"Uhh. Dunno." Billy looked at the floor.

After a long pause, the principal said, "How about if I give you a choice? Choice one: You, your mother, and I can have a conference together to discuss the situation. Choice two: You, Ernesto the Paddle, and I can have a conference together. What do you think?"

"Don't call my mother, please. Anything but that." Billy's cheeks turned bright red.

"Well, then, I guess we have our answer." Principal Peabody smiled a crooked smile.

Shortly thereafter, Billy sat uncomfortably upon his freshly tanned hindquarters in Mrs. Miller's class. At the front of the room, little Sally Turner stood proudly straight and tall. With her dainty clean hands, she held firmly a small white piece of paper. She prepared for an oration.

"As we all know, Sally is this week's Star Student. In accordance with the Star Student rules, her mother has kindly written a letter to the class describing all her wonderful qualities," said Mrs. Miller. "Proceed." She turned to Sally.

In her pretentious high-pitched voice, Sally read the letter:

> Dear Class,
>
>   The Turner Family is very excited that it is Sally's turn to be this week's Star Student. As I am sure you would all agree, the world is blessed to have Sally in it. We feel very lucky to have her in our life. We never have to tell Sally to organize her room or to do her homework. She never complains about going to church on Sunday. She gets straight As in school. She has written her first symphony and intends to conduct it at this year's school Holiday Orchestral Extravaganza. And I am sure you all have heard her play the violin so brilliantly. Oh, and I almost forgot, she is a fantastic ice-skater. We are thinking about the Olympics.
>   We love Sally so very much.
>
> Sincerely,
>
> Mrs. Turner

"Thank you, Sally." Mrs. Miller grinned and nodded her head in agreement. "Now, as is customary, please pick next week's Star Student."

With her snout pointed up, Sally pranced over to the oversized jellybean jar resting on Mrs. Miller's desk. She poked her porcelain hand through the jug's mouth and reached down deep into it. She shuffled the small leaflets of paper with the students' names on them and plucked one out of the glass bucket. She read the name aloud, "Wilhelm Ekkhart von Moosenschmadtenberger the Eighth." In silence, every runny-nosed, pink-faced kid swiveled to gawk at Billy the Bully. He merely turned white.

That night on his unmade bed, a stack of twelve-cent comic books surrounded Wilhelm the Bully. He had just finished reading about Spidey's girlfriend, Gwen, who had just been killed. The Silver Age of comic books had come to an end. He wiped salty tears from his eyes. Threw to the floor the comic book and directed his attention to his mother's latest department store catalog that he swiped from the kitchen. Flipping through its thin black-and-white pages, he quickly came upon his section of interest-the women's undergarments. The geometrical shapes and visual representations of tasty textures absorbed his prepubescent passion. Buxom torpedoes and silky stockings. He examined the engineering applied to intricately designed fasteners, clasps, hooks, straps, snaps, buckles, and zippers. *No, the world was not going to end.* He smiled. *Hope still.*

Then he thought about his mother and the Star Student letter. *Back again. Yes. The world was coming to end.* On his behalf, she would never write such a letter.

Wilhelm only disappointed his stoic, strict, German-bred mother. *He was never good enough. Stout of sinew and cold of heart, her arms were bigger than his legs. Her eyes larger than his hands. And her personality tougher than…well, tougher than anything.*

His mother, Walburga, came from tough German stock. Her father had been a prisoner of war during World War II and had been held by the US military over in Queen Creek at the prisoner of war camp. After the war he obtained a loan from a community bank to purchase a parcel of land on which to raise cotton and a family.

A soft knock at the door interrupted Billy lamenting his Mommy's leer.

"Hey, Squirt, you in there?" Billy's older sister, Christine, glided through the door and lit up the blue room. Billy did not look up. He did not grin to greet her. Just looked at the catalogue pages he perceived as perfect sin. Then, the moment caught him. Embarrassed, he flipped the pages to Toys.

"What's wrong, little buddy?" Her sweet scent lifted his chin. With her hand she brushed back the bangs off his forehead. He looked at her copper wire belt buckle formed into the shape of a peace sign. She wore a purple shirt, lip gloss, and nail polish to match. Through round rose-colored glasses, she viewed him and the earth. She sat next to him. His head fell into her warm bosom and he cried.

"Ahhh. Don't worry, Squirt. Whatever is bothering you, I will help."

And so that night, Christine made everything right. She composed for him a Star Student letter sure to delight:

Dear Class,

As Mrs. Miller looks across the room, I imagine that she is looking across a sky filled with many shining Star Students. Each of you has many special qualities that make you shine in a very special way. When each of your parents looks into that sky with the many shining stars, they immediately recognize their own child's twinkle among all the rest. That feeling that a parent feels when he or she sees his or her own child shine bright is the greatest emotion that a mother or father can feel. That emotion is love. All of your parents love you very much.

For me, when I see Billy's star shine bright, it gives me a joy that I never before imagined that I could feel. When I am sad, he makes me happy. When I am sick, he makes me feel healthy. When I am tired, he gives me energy. I admire his intelligence. Like his grandfather, Billy builds rockets. And he reads. And reads. And reads. He constantly surprises me with his imagination. Billy makes me want to be a better person and a better mom.

I am sure that all of your parents feel the same way about each and every one of you. You are all shining Star Students.

Sincerely,

Mrs. Moosenschmadtenberger

* * *

Young Capricious sat upon her bed. A princess she was. And her bed-a symbol of her sovereign power. From the ceiling, a light valance the color of a desert white rose shielded her and her throne from harsh elements, rogue knights, mythical monsters, hell-breathing dragons, stinging scorpions, and poisonous snakes. The room surrounding her bed was packed full with ladylike accoutrements and glittering necessities. Unfortunately though, the room had become commonplace to her. With her ten-year-old eyes, she looked around and decided that the time had come to ask Daddy to redecorate. Emerald green and azurite blue no longer would do. The simple scheme never expressed her complex condition. She required far more than dual shades. *Ho hum.* She looked glum.

After a soft knock at the door and polite entrance, her older sister stood before her on the earth-toned carpet-covered floor. "What's wrong?" asked Lucy.

"I got a hundred percent on my spelling test." Capricious's eyes filled with a bit of tears.

"That sounds groovy to me. Why are you so sad?"

"I got a hundred percent last week too. Two times. One hundred percent. Karl's been helping me down at Farmers Pond."

"Capricious, that is absolutely fantastic. I am so proud of you. Why are you sad?"

"Mrs. Miller put me on the hard spelling list." From deep down in her throne, Capricious withdrew a piece of paper with the title "Accelerated Spelling List." She held it high-her head and shoulders nestled low into her bright fluffy pillow. Lucy immediately plucked the paper from Capricious's fingers and to it applied profound study. Words with five syllables or more were far too many, twenty in all:

1. Amalgamate
2. Autoregressiveheteroskedasticity
3. Ampullaceous
4. Bacciferous
5. Beneficence
6. Catafalque
7. Chlorofluorocarbon
8. Demagoguery
9. Escutcheon
10. Equestrienne
11. Formaldehyde
12. Hypotenuse
13. Iniquitous
14. Loquacious

15. Metamorphose
16. Opprobrious
17. Pharmaceutical
18. Recalcitrant
19. Sanguinary
20. Triskaidekaphobia

"The test is tomorrow." The pillow muffled Capricious's desperate sound.

Lucy's eyes grew and her heart shrank. "Oh dear. I see. Hmmm. What are we going to do?"

"Mrs. Miller is going to send me to the principal's office for a conference with Ernesto. I just know it."

"You know what?" said Lucy.

"What?" Capricious sat up and wiped her eyes and sniffled her nose.

"We can do this. You can do this. It's not so bad. Don't be sad."

"Really?"

"Really!" Lucy gave Capricious courage.

"Let me tell you a little secret. When you look at this list, it looks kinda daunting. Do you know what daunting means?"

Capricious shook her head.

"Daunting means scary. But, if you look at the list in a different way, it does not look so bad."

"No?"

"No. Let's take just one of the words. Don't worry about the others." Lucy grabbed a number two pencil from atop Capricious's dresser and asked, "Do you like horses?"

"Yes. I love horses." Capricious smiled.

"See this word, *equestrienne*?"

Capricious nodded.

"Well, equestrienne is a fancy name for a horse rider."

"Really?"

"Really. So when you try to remember that word, think of horses."

"OK."

"Now, to spell it, we have to break down the word into little pieces that we can fit together to make the big word. If we think of the word in little pieces and sound it out, it's not as bad."

"Really?"

"Really."

Under the bed's valance, the girls worked into the night. They broke every bit of fright and once again, Capricious achieved one hundred percent again.

* * *

And so it was. The older sisters, Lucy and Christine, helped Capricious and Billy escape the treachery of two terrible twisters.

Stillness

The Sunday morning after the colonel's move into Rancho Opulente, the rising sun pierced through another opening in another set of blinds located just a few streets over from the Hoogeveen's Rancho Opulente residence. The sun heated C.J.'s heavy eyelids and woke her from deep slumber. Her watery eyes had glued themselves shut through the night. As did Karl, C.J. barely had the strength to open her eyes to greet the day. While his physical pain resulted from an overdose of masculine expression moving furniture, she hurt from years of growing and persistent loneliness.

Finally able to peek through one eye, C.J. wondered if the wooden blinds that her husband, Frank, purchased were the cured engineered wood that she had instructed him to buy. They had hired a contractor to install them. But she had forgotten to double-check Frank's purchase order. She knew the intense sun would curl the natural wood if it were not the higher-grade engineered wood. *Time would tell. She wouldn't forget. She would get him if he screwed it up. He never had his head on the family's activities.*

She rolled over in bed and looked at Frank. He knew she had awoken, but he pretended to be asleep. Her husband lacked any desire to speak to her this early in the morning. She kicked her smooth shapely legs to jiggle the bed. *Come on! Wake up! Talk! Respond! Do Something! Anything!* She repeated kicking her legs until she actually kicked him. As he remained still, so did her loneliness, like the stillness before a great storm.

How had she gotten there? Throughout her entire life, men had always fought to be in her presence, to adore her, to shower her with affection. Even then, as a middle-aged married woman, C.J. inevitably attracted men's attention. *How had such an attractive intelligent woman gotten to that lonely place?*

In the past she had maintained soulful connections with many people, both male and female. Most often, only other powerful women demonstrated the capacity, the propensity, and the courage to stand firmly against her strong and complicated character. Only they could relate to her deep perception of the world and her place in it.

In contrast, the word *elemental* characterized C.J's general opinion of men. However much she liked the reassurance powerful men provided, their security had very clearly defined limits. Her emotional and intellectual needs extended far beyond these deficiencies. Additionally, while she enjoyed the comfort of men's physical strength and cognitive reason, she found them predictable and easy to manipulate.

C.J. sighed in disgust at Frank. Rolled over. Then she removed herself from the bed. She proceeded on to her morning routine of exercise and a cool shower. Since it was early in the summer season, the underground pipes and water storage tanks still held cold water. By July the faucets inside the house would only dispense hot water.

Downstairs, Frank remembered that the morning marked exactly one month since he had last made love to C.J. He would be forced to build up his virility for the evening. If he waited any longer than a month, she would think something was wrong. He planned to eat well. Get in a little exercise. Not too much. He would stay away from any alcohol. Figure out some ideas for discussion for that day. Frank would make a list of things that they could discuss. *Yes. Yes. A list.* And he would clean the cat litter box. *She would be so excited.* Then he thought about the Arizona professional baseball team. His excitement grew.

While C.J. was occupied, Frank took the opportunity to escape downstairs without having to speak with her.

He barely reached the first hardwood step before he heard C.J. running on the indoor exercise machine. (Even though she grew up in the desert, and to some extent had gotten used to the extreme temperatures, she still did not enjoy running in the hot morning temperatures outside.) The exercise machine's decibel level indicated her fierce concentration and effort. He shook his head in an attempt to remove the confusion in his skull as he thought of her. His profound inquisitive nature stopped at baseball and corporate politics. While his cerebrum permitted him to forecast the next pitch and his business adversary's next move, his diminished male frontal lobe prevented him from comprehending the complex and beautiful gift that slept next to him at night.

While on the exercise machine, C.J. thought of Karl. He had matured into such a handsome man. She thought about his graceful ability to move mountains of furniture with ease. She remembered his supreme intellect as a boy and the profound gift of learning to read that he had given to her as a child. The memory of his gentle patience with her during her time of tremendous vulnerability gave her goose bumps as she ran. She felt the cool breeze of life blow through her soul. She felt alive. Then C.J. stopped running. *Oh, Karl.*

Frank began his elaborate morning routine as well. He turned on all seven televisions strategically located throughout the first floor. Each varied in size and purpose. Upon a single wall in the great room, Frank had paid the entertainment center designer to mount four widescreens. Arranged together in a square, combined with each television's capability to easily tile four picture frames within its dimensions, Frank could watch sixteen games simultaneously.

In the kitchen he muted the small television's sound such that he could hear *AM Sports Talk Radio* hosted by Herm Sherman. While he watched the scoreboard on the television, he contemplated public baseball debate. From Frank's perspective, life could not get much better as he prepared US state-shaped buttermilk pancakes for the kids.

"Daddy!" Little Lucy bombarded the kitchen. C.J had named her daughter after her older sister.

"Shhhh. One moment, sweetie. Lemme hear the rest of this."

Frank flipped a flapjack with his massive hairy forearms, each measuring greater circumference than his biceps. His great claws reflected his lifelong commitment to hammering a small white ball. Since youth, through childhood, into college, and then onto the three nights a week adult softball league, Frank's arms had put wood to cloth with furious might. His shaggy brown hair and bushy ballplayer mustache accented his athletic build.

"Look at that! Perfectly shaped Florida."

"Daddy. That's not Florida. It's Italy."

"Looks like Florida to me. And since I am the chef, you'll have to accept the fact that this pancake is in the shape of Florida, home of a great Florida baseball team."

"Daddy, it's Italy." Lucy looked up at him.

The skillet began to smoke with burning fry oil. The newly painted light-olive-green wall began absorbing the grease into the varnish and plaster. The odor swirled up to the second floor. Though deep in her thoughts of another time and another place, the scorching fragrance interrupted C.J.'s stream of consciousness and prevented her from achieving her aerobic goal. The machine stopped. Her anger and frustration began.

"Daddy. We've been learning about Italy in school."

"In second grade? Your teacher hasn't even been teaching the states yet. How can you be learning about Italy before you're learning about Florida?"

"Well, Mrs. Brown says that the United States' place in the world is changing. And that we are not the only important country. She says that other countries are just as important as the United States and that someday we may not be a super country."

"You mean superpower."

"Yea. Yea. Mmm hmm. That's right. A superpower."

She kicked a high karate kick. She wore a white martial arts robe with a blood red rising moon and black Chinese symbols on the back. Lucy's older brother, Garrett, countered her kick by striking at her with his own karate chop to her shoulder.

"Well, let me tell you. Your teacher doesn't know what she's talkin' about. The United States will always be number one in the world. We will always be *the* superpower. I am going to write her an e-mail."

"No, Daddy. No. Please don't."

"I'm gonna do it."

"No, Daddy. No."

Frank smiled and winked at her.

"You know, Daddy, everyday I wait in my class for your phone call to come into the room. Every time the phone rings, I just hope it's you coming to have lunch with me. I hope. I hope. I hope."

"They have telephones in the room?"

"Duh, Daddy. Yes. So. When are we having lunch at school?"

"I dunno, Peanut. It's tough. You know I have to work. I have to pay for those karate classes—and your brother's summer soccer and band camp. Which reminds me. Garrett, did they select the band groups for the summer camp yet?"

"Yea. We picked our instruments. You have to sign the permission slip and send the check. It's due tomorrow."

"Which instrument did you pick?"

"Percussion. I am in the B band."

"The B squad?"

"No. Dad. The B band."

"What do you mean, the B squad?"

"No, Dad. You're not listening. It's not like that."

"Am I gonna have to write an e-mail to the band teacher too?"

"She's not a teacher. She's a director."

"Whatever. I wanna hear about the B squad. I'm listening." Frank looked at Garrett with intensity as he continued to pile pancakes shaped like Florida, Georgia, Mississippi, and Montana onto matching light-olive-green breakfast plates.

"Bobby's dad wouldn't let him play tuba."

"Bobby's too small. I wouldn't let 'em play tuba either." Frank chuckled.

"Don't interrupt, Daddy," Lucy scolded.

"Anyway. Bobby switched from tuba to saxophone. But they had too many saxophones. So then she made him play the clarinet instead. And then two other kids switched from trombone and clarinet. And now they moved from the B band to the A band. And I am on the B band."

"What? This does not sound good. What does all of that have to do with you being on the B squad? Why are you not on the A squad?"

"Dad. You're not listening. It's not like that. It's not squads. It's different."

"I'm writing her an e-mail."

"It has nothing to do with first-string and second-string squads," C.J. said as entered the kitchen. "She divided the bands into winds and brass with percussion." C.J. shook her head at Frank. Walked over to the commercial grade gas stove. And turned on the cover fan. "Use the fan! You're burning the pancakes."

"How the hell would I know all that crap?"

"See the fan switch? Just turn it to *on*!"

"Not the fan. The band crap!"

"It's not crap, Daddy."

"Life is competition, I am sorry to say. There is first place and then there is everything below that. If you're not first, or A squad, you're nothing. I don't care if she calls them 'winds' or whatever. I am writing an e-mail, and I am going to have her rename the squads. Garrett will *not* be on 'B' anything! And that's *final!*"

Frank considered himself to be on the A squad of life. He lived in Rancho Opulente, and he worked in a corner office. Frank served as executive vice president of business development, western region, at Rally's Sporting Goods Corporation. His father was on the board of directors and several years ago suggested strongly to middle management that his *well-qualified* son be introduced to the hiring process.

As C.J. listened to Frank pontificate about being number one, she remembered the first time she ever saw him—close to fifteen years previous. A furry fellow wearing a florescent yellow and green surfing tank top had been staring at her all night long. Every guy had been gawking at her, but not in the same manner in which Frank looked at her. Under the Beach Bar and Grill's rooftop and within the sweaty sea of flesh-seeking inebriated San Diego State students, Frank's inorganic stare sent C.J. into an uncomfortable fidget. Neither vulnerable female passersby nor howling beer buddies failed to draw his attention away from his target.

Not for two hours did his mechanical mannerism deter. By evening's end, liquid courage drew C.J. to confront her small fear of Frank. She stumbled through a bevy of bystanders to meet the odd man behind the stare. As she approached him, he did not blink. Preempting her first slurred speech, he asked, "Could you move to the left?" C.J. turned around and discovered a big-screen television located across the dance floor behind the table where she and her friends had been seated. Frank had been watching the television (not her) all night. The scoreboard broadcasting across its screen had forever been embedded into her memory.

Her mind back in the present, C.J. looked back at Frank finishing his triumphant thoughts on the necessity of being first. She said, "On August 26, 1989, during the Little League World Series Championship, the US National Little League team from Trumball, Connecticut, defeated the Kang-Tu Little League team from Kaohsiung, Taiwan, five to two in Williamsport, Pennsylvania."

Frank stood surrounded by his family in the olive-green kitchen, stunned and speechless. Then a flash of brilliance came to him. *That was it! Fantastic. Expounding her sports statistic relieved him of his duty to think up a list of romantic conversational topics for the day...for the month! Why had he not thought of it before? They could talk about baseball all day, and then he could make love to her at night. No need to clean the cat litter.*

Storm Front

Two young girls, both barely able to see over the perfume counter, poked their noses above the glass. The bouquet of European scents filled the air, attracting all who passed by the perfume and cosmetics department. Through layers of dark mascara and eyeliner, the exotic-looking saleswoman dressed in black glared down upon the two. She forced herself to fake a smile.

"May I help you?"

"I'm first!" said the older of the two.

C.J.'s daughter, Lucy, pushed aside three-year-old Emily, who lived down the street from C.J. and her family. Lucy used all of her tiny might to pull herself up onto the high chair in front of the intricately shaped samples and multi-colored makeup.

"Nooooo. Noooo. I first!" Screaming, Emily pulled Lucy down from the plush white leather stool.

This shrill scream sent chills through patrons and perfume pushers. Everyone looked. The tall saleswoman's smile turned down to a frown.

"Lucy! Please." C.J. crumbled with embarrassment. "Lucy, you are older than her. She is only three. Let her go first. Please! Don't cause a scene."

"No! I'm first!" Lucy's eyebrows straightened with determination.

"No! I first! I first!" Emily held firm.

"Lucy, this is her first time here. You've been here lots of times. And besides, she doesn't understand. Just let her go first."

"No. I'm first."

"I first! I first!" Tears poured from Emily's eyes.

C.J.'s face turned bright red. She looked at the saleswoman and apologized. Two older rich-looking women on the other side of the counter impatiently walked away. The saleswoman turned stone-cold angry and clenched her fists and teeth.

"Is there a problem here?" A smooth low-toned male voice broke the tension. Karl Hoogeveen smiled and stood up straight. All four ladies—the two kids, C.J., and the Diamond's Department Store salesperson—stared at King Karl. Emily stopped crying. Karl wore a thick, pressed, white-collared shirt—open at the top. His shiny leather belt and platinum buckle hung loosely around his tight waist. The expensive slacks dangled perfectly over his fine leather cordovan shoes.

"What's your name, pretty girl?" Karl winked and smiled.

"Emily," she replied, sniffling uncontrollably.

"And yours?" He looked at C.J.'s daughter and turned his head gracefully.

"Lucy," she said.

"Well. I have an idea. How about if I move that chair from the other counter over there and bring it here so that both of you can be first? What do you think?"

Both little ladies nodded with shy smiles. Karl's baby blues, fancy threads, and tender tone lulled the adults into quiet relaxation too.

After Karl glided across the floor and relocated the opposing chair into position, he sat both delighted girls next to each other.

"There, now. This is going to work. Everybody is number one." Karl looked at the saleswoman. "What's your name?" He smiled and lifted one eyebrow in her direction. The dark-haired woman looked stunned and did not respond.

"Her name is Sasha. Says right there on her name tag." C.J. looked at Karl. "Can't you read?" She smiled.

Karl grinned. "*Touché.*"

C.J. looked back at him, smiling nervously. Their eyes met.

"Are you going to buy something?" Sasha asked.

"You are quite the closer, aren't you? They teach you that at sales training?" Karl looked annoyed.

"Well, I just don't want to be wasting my time while other paying customers are walking away," said the saleswoman.

"What's your coworker's name over there?"

"That's Mary."

"Could you be so kind as to ask Mary to step over here, please?"

While Sasha marched over to Maria, the two little girls and C.J. eagerly looked at Karl. They all listened to Maria and Sasha's heels clicking the floor as the two salespersons returned to the counter.

"How can I help you?" Maria smiled.

"We are very longtime loyal customers interested in your fine products. However, we are not interested in working with Sasha. I would like to leave open a line of credit for these two pretty girls to pick and choose whatever they desire."

Karl advanced his credit card to Maria. He thought about the fact that he could not afford this extravagant gesture. He thought about the air-conditioning repair bill, his speeding ticket, Sven's soccer club dues, Karla's tumbling class tuition, Nineveh's college tuition, Sven's emergency room bill, his brother's bail, their upcoming anniversary, the summer vacation...And then he looked at C.J. And then he smiled. His troubles were far, far away. Sasha stomped off. Her snooty demeanor had caused her to lose this sale to her coworker.

"How is it that a moving man can afford this?" C.J. looked skeptical.

"It's Memorial Day. See the sign?" Karl pointed to the weekend sales event. "And...I'm not exactly a moving man."

"Then what are you?"

Karl leaned into C.J., just as he had done at Farmers Pond years ago. He tucked his nose into the lush curls above her ear and whispered, "I'm Karl." He extended his tanned hand.

C.J. blushed. She remembered the day on the *Goodyear Frogger.* The day he had first whispered his name to her. Karl gently held her soft hand in his. She regained composure and pulled back.

"It's a pleasure to meet you, Karl. I'm Capricious Jo Harmony." She pretended not to know him. She feared the consequences of disclosure to the world—to her daughter. Someone in the store would see her expression. Would know her true feelings.

"I think your girls are happy," Karl said. He understood and felt much the same.

"You seem pretty good at making women happy." C.J. looked skeptical. Scared.

"Only the pretty ones." Karl winked.

"Oh, Karl," C.J. whispered.

C.J. blushed again when she remembered the silent emotion they had exchanged days before, when the colonel had moved into Rancho Opulente. A sinking feeling fell over C.J. It tied her stomach into a knot. She swallowed. Her throat hurt. *Why did she feel this way?* A weak smile barely masked her anxiety. *What did he think?*

Karl too felt weak. He responded to the sight, the sound, and the smell of C.J. His normally strong, slow, rhythmic breathing and heartbeat escaped him. His midsection tightened and constricted. Experience commanded him to relax. He concentrated on his respiratory system. He breathed slowly again. Then he awoke from his meditation and absorbed the beauty before him.

Amid the bouquet of fragrance swirling around them, Karl smelled C.J.'s flesh. He sensed that she he had just come into the air-conditioned store from the Arizona heat outdoors. A misty chemical compound comprised of C.J.'s sweat and the expensive body sprays and women's cologne she wore cut its way through the air and into Karl. She found her way inside him. He wished to find his way into her. Karl reached out to her and cupped her elbow gently with his palm.

"I have something for you," he said.

"Really?"

Cosmetics occupied the attention of the two girls, and the rest of the world seemed so far away. C.J. threw caution to the wind and touched Karl's forearm. They came together like the collision of two weather patterns, forming a passionate tropical storm front. Their dizzying emotions whirled around them.

In the eye of the storm, Karl said, "I wrote you something. Do you want to read it?"

The two stopped touching and parted.

"Yes," she said with a bright red face. She was delighted that he too had been thinking about her.

Karl loved to hear C.J. say yes. The intonation of her voice danced through his inner ear. The tone pleased him. He stepped toward her. As he looked into her big chocolate- and vanilla-colored eyes, his peripheral vision brought into his detailed analysis the rest of her incredible combination: her bushy brown waves of hair reaching down just between her shoulder blades; the red earrings that matched her shiny lipstick; her painted fingernails; her tight-fitting blue skirt; and her pointed red leather shoes. Her tasteful white blouse completed the rest of her Memorial Day red, white, and blue ensemble. Through the light material, he saw her undergarment's white lace beneath. She reminded him of a World War II USO poster girl. Again with his peripheral vision, he followed her body's contours and assessed the parabolic shape of her bosom. Karl handed C.J. his little note.

> My eyes are blue; but behind them, my thoughts are the devil's red. In this moment, happy tortured thinking plagues me. Of course, I am thinking of you. In this desert heat, my thoughts are far away. I am thinking of you and me in the Andes Mountains—of arriving in Santiago, Chile—of catching a sketchy bus that winds up a traitorous mountain to a ski resort designed by French architects. I am thinking of a cocoon-shaped restaurant carved into the earth beneath the roots of a huge exotic South American spruce tree—a restaurant that illuminates the night amid dark snow. Are you thinking of me? Are you thinking about where it snows in August? About where it snows in September? I am thinking about sheepskin-covered seats that keep occupants warm during cold, cuddly nights. I can smell—I can feel—the glow of the crackling fire. I can taste the Argentinean wine. Tell me, Capricious. Do I taste you?

"Oh, Karl. I don't know what to say." C.J. bowed her now-heavy head to the floor. *When had he written the note? Why did he appear out of nowhere to give it to her?*

Then her daughter shouted, "I want red, white, and blue paint. Different colors for each finger and toe." She stipulated her patriotic holiday requirements. Lucy continued, "And I want a flag sticker on my thumb and big toe. On the left toe, I want the revolutionary flag with only thirteen stars. The right toe, I want a Yankee Civil War flag. On my thumbs, I'll take the flag sticker with all fifty states!"

"Sweetie, I don't think we have the older flag stickers. I think we just have the one with fifty states," Maria the salesperson said, trying to be diplomatic.

"Ohhhh. Are you sure? That's not good enough. I want the other ones. Don't you too, Emily?"

"Yes. Me too! I want what she wants."

"Well, I am not sure what to do. We only have the flag with fifty states." Maria the salesperson looked perplexed.

C.J. leaned over to Karl and whispered, "I think we have another problem with the girls and the stickers." She smiled.

"Not sure that I can fix this one."

"Lucy! You're just gonna have to take the sticker she has. She doesn't have the other ones that you want," said C.J.

"Aww. I wanted the other ones too. But OK."

Lucy jumped off the chair. Executed a perfect cartwheel. She launched herself up into the scented atmosphere to throw two karate punches and a double high kick.

She turned to Maria at the counter and cheered, "Red, white, and blue! You got it! You got it! Red, white, and blue! You got it! Cause that's the way I roll!"

Little Lucy won the gathering crowd's approval. Everyone roared and clapped. Though C.J. never expressed herself so gregariously, her daughter had certainly inherited her innate power over people.

As Maria directed Lucy and Emily over to the huge leather lounge chair pedicure station, Karl invited C.J. to join them.

"I'm happy to throw a pedicure for your feet onto the credit card as well. Even your feet are pretty, Capricious." Karl grinned.

C.J.'s face again turned bright red. A heat rash flamed across her chest and up her neck. She smiled to cover her awkwardness. Her white teeth gleaned under the store's energy-efficient florescent lights.

Karl appreciated her reaction to his words and his note. He had taken a bit of a chance revealing too much of himself. Since the day he had written it, he had carried it with him, hoping to see her again. By chance, he had walked into Diamond's Department Store that day.

Capricious liked his unique perception. Of course, throughout her lifetime a million male souls had bravely, or perhaps stupidly, tossed upon her countless love notes. But in her wake lay tangled and tormented torsos masticated by her attitude. Certainly, Karl was not among these floating masculine carcasses.

With wiggly toes high in the air, the kids snickered as Maria instructed two middle-aged Vietnamese women wearing white lab coats and synthetic fiber face masks to embark upon the pedicure proceedings.

"I insist," Karl commanded C.J. "Have a seat next to your daughter. You deserve it."

C.J.'s awkward red rash still glowed. Maria noticed it. Then Maria looked at Karl with despise. Karl winked back at Maria. Maria could not prevent her blush either. As C.J. momentarily became jealous of Maria having Karl's attention, Karl turned his interest to seating C.J. As she snuggled her shapely hindquarters into the chair and situated safely her dyed-blue lizard-skin purse, Karl knelt down and removed her shoes with his tender muscular left hand. He looked to see that Lucy and Emily were preoccupied with the Vietnamese ladies and that they were unaware of his intent. Karl knew enough not to be too demonstrative with his affections, as young girls tended be free speaking with their daddies.

"I have something else for you, C.J.," said Karl. He handed her the emerald charm bracelet she had lost in Mrs. Miller's classroom years ago as a child. As he fastened the bracelet around her muscular and toned wrist, C.J. sat motionless in shock before regaining her composure.

"Karl, this is the bracelet my older sister gave me before…before…before…you know. Where did you find this?" she asked.

"You remember stuck-up Sally Turner from Mrs. Miller's class? After you moved away from Goodyear, I saw her wearing it. I knew it was yours, so I took it back. I kept it for you, hoping to someday return it."

Confident in the conditions conducive to his desire, Karl placed his left hand under C.J.'s slim bare foot and began massaging her. He hit the spot where bone, tissue, and the weight of each day inexorably joined beneath her. His hand's pulsating rhythm untied one strand at a time the clutch of loneliness that her marriage had weaved into her vertebrae. Conflicted, she knew the canons of morality stipulated that she should resist. C.J. cast aside any hope of probity. She closed her eyes to feel the tears roll down the sides of her face and her loneliness slip away.

Karl thought about the prospect of kissing her, but rejected the idea for fear of public ridicule. Instead, through touch alone he swallowed her soul with his affectionate hand.

Smack!

"You get out of here!" One of the Vietnamese pedicurists hit him over the head with an oversized coarse-grade wooden nail file.

"Get out of here!"

Both C.J. and Karl laughed uncontrollably as C.J. wiped the tears from her face.

"I should go," he said. Karl grinned and winked at C.J. She returned a sly secret smile.

For the duration of the trio's foot treatment, C.J. could think of nothing but the bliss into which Karl had momentarily dunked her. No human being had ever made her feel anything so pleasurable. Since the beginning of time, mankind has infinitely expressed this emotion. Perhaps her dominance over the individuals around her prevented her from experiencing one of life's greatest gifts. Whether upon the walls of caves or the ceilings of cathedrals, C.J. had always been one to observe and appreciate the expression, but not one to fully understand it—until the moment the man from her past laid his hand upon her bare foot.

Karl, on the other hand, understood the emotion. Beneath his brawny pelt, a desperate romantic throbbed. While leaving Diamond's Department Store, he too savored the memory of the moment that had just passed. As he walked, he perceived his surroundings in two dimensions, not three. Karl's acuity of the present escaped him. Only the thought of C.J. reclining in the pedicure throne persisted. On his palm he still sensed the warmth of her skin. In his spine he still sensed her soul. *Oh, C.J.*

Monsoon

However successful conservative religious groups behind closed doors succeeded to censor Rancho School District academic literature (they placed *The Adventures of Tom Sawyer, To Kill A Mockingbird, Catcher In The Rye* and many other American classics on a banned booklist), they failed to contain Harry Jester and his fishing followers at the pond. While church elders quietly advised puppet school board members to mandate district policies without true public debate, they struggled to implement Rancho Opulente Association bylaws to eliminate alcohol in and around Rainbow Rapids, its pond, and the neighborhood recreational parks. At every relevant association meeting, Harry the Fisherman always rallied his plebian base to block any and all attempts to encroach upon good old-fashioned fun.

"Harry!" shouted a clean-cut thirty-something man poking his head through the partially rolled-down window of his two-year-old silver minivan. "I just got off work!" he blasted. The man wore a collared pink shirt, a dark red striped tie, and a navy-blue name tag that read "Christopher—Store Manager." "I got off early! I'll be back in a couple of minutes after I do a few chores for my wife."

Christopher could barely contain himself. He had for weeks anticipated a 2008 Memorial Day celebration with Harry. Harry waved and nodded while he tied flies to three kids' leader lines at the sparkling blue water pond's shoreline. Christopher sped off in his cube-shaped auto but never returned.

Behind Harry and the kids, families gathered together carrying colorful bags, white Styrofoam chests filled with ice-cold beverages, and aluminum-foil-covered paper plates piled high with flavorful food. An Argentinean ice-cream vendor circled them in his musical sweet-smelling vehicle. Beyond the park's picnic tables, a carnival of squeaky rides and barely visible blinking lights roared beneath the desert sun. Shady characters from distant places lured passersby with games of impossible chance, fresh cumulus nimbus clouds of cotton candy, and oversized, caramel-covered, sour, green apples. Children screamed. Men laughed. Women gossiped.

As their children fished with Harry, C.J., Mrs. Andersen, and Mrs. Florence huddled in the protective shade provided by one of the clay-tiled roof-covered picnic areas adjacent to the pond. Four years had passed since

C.J. had seen Karl. Off and on she had thought about him. But she fell into the routine of living as one of the First Ladies of Rancho Opulente. On that holiday, the trio participated in the time-honored tradition of people watching. They studied a young porcelain-skinned woman walking by them. All three heads turned in the direction of the dark-haired woman wearing dull silver six-inch-high platform pumps and a white T-shirt embroidered with loud glittery letters that declared "Rancho Premier Boys Soccer Club." With her powdered nose held high in the air, she stomped unknowingly into a pile of fresh fish tripe. C.J. wondered if the woman's heavy cheap perfume would disguise the stink.

"Hey, isn't that Julie?" Mrs. Florence tried to wave to her.

"She saw you. I am sure of it. She didn't wave back!" C.J. scrunched her eyebrows. "I thought you two were friends."

"I thought we were too."

"So what happened?"

"Well. Timmy didn't make the premier soccer team this year. We ended up on the select team."

"The B squad?" asked C.J.

"Yes. The B squad."

"So what? Who cares?" Mrs. Andersen interjected.

"Evidently, Julie cares. She hasn't spoken to me since they made the premier team and we didn't."

"You're kidding?"

"Nope. I am serious. Premier families don't speak to select families." Mrs. Florence shook her head, smiling and rolling her eyes.

"Well. For what it's worth, she looks like white trash in that outfit."

"I don't understand how her Brett made the team and my Timmy didn't. Tim is better than Brett."

"So says Tim's mom. Sure you're not biased?" C.J. questioned Mrs. Florence's objectivity.

"No. No. Her Brett's not that good. He is the slowest kid on the team. His footwork isn't there. And he is always out of position. He doesn't belong on the premier team. Last year the coach played Tim far more than he put Brett into the games."

"I know how he made the team!" exclaimed Harry as he returned from the pond to his ice chest brimming with the day's beer supply. He crushed an empty aluminum can. Tossed it into the trash receptacle and reached for another. As he popped its tab and sprayed ale into the hot atmosphere, he explained further his assertion. "Nigel Caruthers is the coach of that premier team. Right?" he asked. The women nodded in agreement. "The guy with the English accent," clarified Harry. They nodded again.

"I hate to break this to you, but he ain't English. And his real name ain't Nigel Caruthers. His name is Burt somethin'. That act of his is only for the benefit of you Rancho parents."

"How do you know all of this?" asked Mrs. Florence.

"I got drunk with him over at the Snake Pit."

"That disgusting strip joint?"

"The gentlemen's club. Exactly. You all think paying a few thousand bucks in soccer fees pays for an English soccer coach. American coaches just ain't good enough for you folks. Burt understands all of that, and he plays right into what you want. He said for years he couldn't get hired by any of the good-paying clubs...until he switched to the accent and the new name."

"That's very interesting. But what does that have to do with Julie's kid making the team?" Mrs. Andersen wanted to be in the know.

Harry burped. "Sorry," he said. Then guzzled back half the can he had just opened. He burped again and said, "Sorry." With a fancy light-green kitchen towel stained with fish blood, he wiped the sweat off his forehead. "Burt banged her," he declared.

In unison all three women shouted, "*What?*"

"Yea. Burt banged that broad. Or should I say, she banged Burt. He told me she was on top. Anyhow, that's how that kid got on the team."

"Unbelievable!" Mrs. Florence stood up and paced around in a small circle. "The premier team is that important to her. She doesn't care about Brett. She cares about winning and being first at everything!"

"Life's a competition," C.J said as she shook her head. She thought of her husband, Frank.

Harry drank the rest of the beer in the can. Belched and grabbed another. Mrs. Florence noticed someone had engraved Harry's name into the picnic table closest to the pond. Spread across *his* table he had laid his Byzantine angler's arsenal. The dazzling array of synthetic flies organized into countless clear little bait boxes intimidated Mrs. Florence. The depth of his passion for fishing became clear to her.

"I'm telling you, the egrets are eating all of the small minnows. Look over there! A whole flock of them are circling over there."

Bob, Harry's buddy, appeared from the crowd, and he pointed to the covey. In one hand he carried a bloody cutting board. In the other hand, he held a long fishing knife. He cleared a space upon Harry's table and organized his live minnow bait.

"Throw me a beer, would ya, Harry?"

Bob began butchering the minnows into small bite-size pieces intended for hook and bobber.

"I told you I am using flies. Aren't you going to enter the Desert Angler Affiliation Fly-Fishing Tournament?" asked Harry.

"Nope. Not me." Bob refused.

A breeze parted C.J.'s bangs. She ignored the small slaughter occurring next to her. Instead she enjoyed the calming affect of the location. She acknowledged the fact that Harry basically lived here in this man-made retreat, away from it all. She saw stuffed into one of his satchels a dusty old faded blue book, *The Brothers Karamazov* by Fyodor Mikhaylovich Dostoyevsky. For a moment C.J. wondered what it would be like to step completely out of her life and into Rainbow Rapids fishing and world literature. *Perhaps Harry knew something the rest of us didn't.* She thought about stepping into a new blissful life with Karl. *What would it be like to be completely fulfilled emotionally? What would it be like to be passionately in love?*

But, no. These thoughts were wrong. In the fullness of time, C.J. embraced her life and everything in it. She was proud of her family and of her accomplishments. She thought of Lucy and Garrett. Then she smiled.

"The translation's bad!" Harry slurped at his beer. He had noticed C.J. staring at his book.

"I'm sorry. What?" C.J. asked.

"The translation. Fyodor was Russian. That copy was published about a hundred years ago. It was handed down to me from my great-grandmother," Harry said as held down a burp.

"I would be happy to loan you my modern translation," said C.J. She surprised Harry.

"No. No. That's not necessary."

Before heading back down to the pond, Harry selected three more flies from his boxes and pinned them onto his weather-beaten hat. He belched again and smiled to himself regarding the dichotomy he so purposely presented—being so intellectual and simultaneously repulsive in the presence of Rancho's First Ladies.

C.J. watched him. She began thinking of the upcoming *Rancho Opulente* fly-fishing tournament. *Harry seemed to know what he was doing.* With a natural fluid motion, he whipped his fishing line back over and above his head, then forward gently to rest its fly hook upon the water. For a moment he permitted the feathery-looking fly to float on the surface before he snapped it back again over his head. The bright orange-colored line danced above him like a sparkling, winding, desert wind kicking up magic dust. Below the florescent funnel, Harry waved it with his artistic touch. C.J. wondered if anyone could paint such a picture in the sky and on the water. Within moments he drew a large fish up into his beautiful torrent and onto his hook.

Harry reeled it ashore and held his catch high above the crowd of kids beneath him. After a rush of frenzied envy and joy, the crew of little people returned to their happy task. Each child clumsily hammered his own casting interpretation into the sky and then onto the water. None pledged the prodigious hope of a natural fly-fisherman that Harry had promised some forty years previous. But neither the fish nor the mob cared in which pattern the plastic flies flew. Ultimately, Harry's complement of children succeeded to pull ashore plenty of rainbow trout and bigmouth bass. The fish were farm raised by Karl Hoogeveen at the Rainbow Rapids River Technology and Fish Farm Company.

While the ladies' discourse churned with gossip, they kept surveying Memorial Day activities. Harry gathered up his troops from the pond and relocated them upstream to Rainbow Rapids. Fully constructed with modern ingenuity, the mile-long river encircled Rancho Opulente Park. During its creation, geological surveyors ensured the accuracy of the three-percent grade and the density of the relocated freshly compacted soil. Hydraulic engineers and fabricators installed huge water pumps and pipes beneath the ground that continually pushed water from the pond back up to the top of the river. Farm fisheries stocked it with genetically selected hungry fish. Latin American landscape workers wearing collared teal shirts and pleated khaki pants ensured its lush banks. Karl was the technological mastermind behind it all.

Harry insisted that each young man find his own spot along the river's edge, each having sufficient distance from the next as not to snag the other with rogue flying hooks. He effortlessly disentangled the braided chaos of kids into a finely tuned fisher symphony. Innately he knew both the children and the fish and easily directed both groups, merging them into one harmonious event.

Critical rapids roared past. An almost-still hot breeze gently teased the Palo Verde trees around them. The boys' learning lines whipped with uncoordinated gracefulness. All hoped for a tug. When hooked, powerful fighting fish sprinted back and forth on the lines with tenacious attitude. Tired petite hands reeled light metallic wheels, pulling prey to hand. Young fishermen screamed. Harry hooted. Moms smiled.

"Look how happy the kids are." All the moms' hearts filled with joy.

"Look!" Mrs. Florence pointed in the other direction back across the pond to the street.

A group of elderly World War II veterans sat in the back of a long brightly painted racing motorboat with flames running down both port and starboard sides. The nearly forty-foot boat rested on its trailer, while three younger couples rode in the king cab of a cherry red dually pickup truck pulling the rig. On the back of the new truck, three stickers decorated the bumper: (1) "Don't Take My Guns, My Money, or My Freedom"; (2) "No Silly, Paychecks Are for Workers"; and (3) "Desert Christian Church."

The driver slowly maneuvered the truck and its load up over the street curb onto the thick, dark-green easement grass bordering the pond. As the boat bumped back and forth, the women watched the dark navy blue-and-gold-lettered World War II Memorial hats above bobbing back and forth in the boat's white cushioned open cockpit. The motion gave one of the white hairs a flashback to his heroic 1944 Normandy Beach landing and liberation.

"What the heck are they doing?"

"They're not going to try to put the boat in the pond water. Are they?"

"No. I don't think so. Looks like they've just parked it on the shoreline."

"Oh, look. They're gonna fish off the side of that thing." All three women laughed hysterically.

"Those young people look like newlyweds. Wonder where they got the money for that big toy?" C.J. posed the question.

"Well, either father-in-law kicked in, or they did what everybody else is doing."

Mrs. Florence looked at Mrs. Andersen and both said, "Refinancing the house!"

Home prices had risen steadily and rapidly during that period. Much of the community had been living above their means by pulling equity cash out of their homes through easy-to-obtain lender-encouraged restructured mortgages. The properties and the ever-rising home prices collateralized the loans.

"We did it," Mrs. Andersen confessed. "It was a bit of a stretch. But we paid off all of our credit cards, bought two cars, upgraded the interior of the house, and went to Europe for three weeks."

Ahead of the women way off in the distance, the sky filled with an ominous brown cloud moving quickly along the floor of the Sonoran Desert's Valley of the Sun. Originating from Mexico, the seasonal reversing wind flew over Gila River and past South Mountain to the City of Chandler. After moving over a newly constructed freeway, three dry canals, and a small airport, the storm system approached Rancho Opulente.

Back up the river on an artificial perch, C.J.'s son, Garrett, caught site of the squall and laid down his junior-sized fishing pole. He had never seen before such a mile-high wall of thick dust. From far away it seized his attention. He watched it consume one neighborhood after another: Desert Hills Estates, Quiet Canyon, Saguaro Heights, Crystal Lakes, and many more. The storm moved quickly across the valley until it reached Rancho Opulente. The boy saw the egrets circling over the pond abandon their feast and fly away.

"Monsoon! Monsoon! Monsoon!" The crowd yelled with fear.

In less than sixty seconds, the sun disappeared. The wind blew steadily at sixty miles an hour and hurled thick eye-piercing desert dust. Its victims ran in vain to take cover. Weak (over-watered) trees bent, then uprooted from soft soil. Red, white, and blue tents catapulted across the park. Muddy rain and desert dirt-colored bullets of hail formed from dust and water bombarded the innocent and the semi-worldly beneath.

As quickly as it had arrived, the desert storm passed. In the aftermath it left hundreds of stunned casualties stricken wet and dirty; the motorboat covered in mud; and

WWII hats scattered about. Emerging from the decimated riverbank, Harry and his kids laughed as they looted the bounty of caramel apples strewn all over the park.

C.J. looked at Mrs. Andersen and said, "I thought the colonel's wife said there weren't any bad hair days in the desert." All three women chuckled, even though their picnic had been destroyed. Without a word further, they joined the rest of the sullied folks and began the cleanup.

* * *

The monsoon had dumped several cubic yards of sand and dust into Colonel Wiley's pool. The colonel wanted to speak to the new pool man. He had only spoken to the guy on the phone. The pool man's family making noises in the background during the call had made an impression upon the colonel. *A family man was always reliable.* Additionally, all the other pool service men refused to meet customers on Sundays. The colonel appreciated the guy's enthusiasm to get started on a new account by meeting him on a Sunday. He looked at his watch and figured he would meet the pool man out front. Perhaps this first encounter would serve as a measure of promptness.

Precisely thirty seconds from the top of the hour, Colonel Wiley heard a clunky engine rattle up the hill to the front of his home. The small rusty and faded yellow twenty-year-old pickup truck's tires appeared bald. None of the four wheels rolled straight. Crooked and worn pool implements hung over the side of the truck bed. A torn and brown stained blue pool net lay across an empty chemical carton. Back in the eighties, the pool guy had used a stolen retail store price gun to create the company logo displayed on the side of the truck: "GE RGE THE PO L DUDE. LICE SED AND BONDED." The colonel gained no confidence from the missing letters.

"Good morning, George."

"Good morning, sir."

Under his wide-brimmed straw hat, George smiled to reveal the tobacco chew between his dingy teeth, highlighted by his cigarette-stained brown and grey mustache. George continued, "This is a perfect account for me. It's right on my way home. I can swing by on my way to my other accounts. And it's a new pool, so it won't require much work. This is perfect."

The colonel looked dumbfounded.

"Why don't we go around back to take a peek at 'er?" George broke the silence.

From above on the second floor, the colonel's neighbor, Professor Bader Al-Ajeel, observed George and the colonel. As the two below walked around to the back of the colonel's house, Bader proceeded into the bathroom to begin his morning shower. A newly tenured professor of earth science at State, Professor Al-Ajeel observed every opportunity to conserve energy and the earth's limited resources. Against his oil-rich Kuwaiti family's objections, he abandoned fossil fuels and devoted his life to saving the earth. He had a special water reclamation sprinkler system installed into the landscape around the house. He and his family did not drink water from plastic disposable bottles. Instead, they used a filtered water system. He drove his bike or walked whenever possible. The family purchased a hybrid car and placed solar energy panels up on the roof. When he showered, he collected in a bucket the dirty shower water and then used it to flush the toilet. By his calculation he saved a few gallons of water a day.

Bader Al-Ajeel paused his morning shower to observe his neighbor and the pool man below. He opened the window a crack to eavesdrop on the conversation. On the windowsill sat a dark framed colorful photo of him and his brother racing dusty camels around the family palace in Kuwait. And so he listened.

"Looks to me like the water is pretty bad out of balance. It's gonna take a lot of work to get it back." George scratched his head. "Not sure about this. We have a few options."

"Like what?" Again the colonel looked dumbfounded.

"Well, the easiest thing to do would be to just drain the pool and start fresh by refilling it with new water. How many gallons you got in there?"

"Eighteen thousand, six hundred and thirty-two." The colonel had recently read the owners documentation that came with the pool.

"Yea. I say we just drain it and fill it right back up again."

"What's the water bill gonna be, you think?"

"Not more than a couple a hundred bucks or so. It's nothin'."

Professor Al-Ajeel's heart ventricles shuttered, then pounded and strained with irregularity. He estimated that if he conserved three gallons of water a day, it would take him approximately eighteen years to offset the colonel's single pool draining. Such thoughts left his countenance coiled in sorrowful contraction.

Beneath the professor, the colonel looked up at his Kuwaiti neighbor. Bader heard the colonel say quietly to George, "I got me a rag-head camel jockey neighbor." Both men sniggered and proceeded out to the front of the house to finalize the details of pool maintenance. Bader shut the window in disgust.

After George departed, the colonel returned inside to sit in his large soft leather chair situated in the corner of the trophy room. He sipped eighteen-year-old scotch from a small crystal glass engraved with his initials and read the fancy gold and silver label on the face of the liquor bottle. Its intricate description of "complex" flavors reinforced the value of the bottle's contents and furthermore, the colonel's own self worth. He inhaled smoke from the end of the cigarette butt that he held in his other hand. The action stung his lungs. In seconds, nicotine seared a temporary slight dizzy sensation into his brain. He savored the taste of expensive whiskey and a cheap cigarette as he exhaled. A plume of smoke drifted up from the foul-smelling hole in his face into the vent embedded into the high ceiling above him. The smoke travelled through the air ducts, past a scorpion chasing a grasshopper, and into his daughter's bedroom. The colonel down below ignored her chronic cough. Instead, on that Memorial Day weekend as he did every Memorial Day weekend, he thought of his experience in Vietnam and of his brave companions with whom he served. He remembered their ultimate sacrifice. For a moment, he felt guilty. *Of his five closest comrades, why was he the only one to have survived?* Lost in thought, he also ignored the creaking sound coming from the chair's wooden frame upon which he lounged. The weight of his belly and doughy muscles strained one of the chair's wooden joints. Having relocated from the dense moist air on the California Coast, the chair's hard oak bent, twisted, and cracked as it dried in the desert climate. The colonel reclined, shattering the chair's brittle joint. His fungus-infested feet, his yellow drink, and his fire-coaled cigarette all rocketed upward as his head crash landed on the hard floor. The force of gravity pulled toward him a wave of whiskey and white-hot cigarette ember. The colonel grunted in pain. The shock of the event and the dizziness then passed. He opened his raisin eyes and looked up. The great blue swordfish trophy stared down upon him from its high position upon the eggshell-colored wall. The colonel's prize hung crookedly on its mounting brackets. It teetered precariously. He frowned.

TSUNAMI

JUNE 2008

Soon after Memorial Day, the earth's Northern Hemisphere pointed ever closer to the sun. Arizona shadow's shrunk. Days grew longer. And the ground hardened beneath newly formed grey asphalt steamrolled by mostly men and some women all wearing bright orange vests and matching hard hats. Phoenix thrived amidst signs warning "Fines Doubled In Construction Zones." Over the course of just a few years, activities called "progress" brought an unanticipated consequence. Despite homes and buildings erected with advanced energy-efficient materials and technologies, the desert valley's vast topology transformed into a grid comprised of heat-holding tar and cement. The average daily temperature in Phoenix rose. Nights no longer cooled the days' blaze. Air-conditioners pumped cool air longer and harder. Civic engineers had overlooked the thermal characteristics of the primary building material used to construct the new modern valley. Phoenix was hotter than it was ever before.

Within this bake, Karl thought of C.J. One night he sat sweating next to the little man-made lake. He fantasized about C.J. as she stood across Rancho Opulente's pond at the mouth of Rainbow Rapids. They had not seen each other in four years. He thought about her shake. Her wiggle. Her model and make. Karl observed her bait the hook at the end of her daughter Lucy's fishing line. The child's Pink Princess fishing pole sparkled beneath artificial lamplights illuminating the pond's boardwalk.

"Hey, Dad! I think I caught one!" Karl's son, Sven, interrupted Karl as he panted predatorily at C.J.

"Reel him in, son. Not too hard. Gentle but firm. He's all yours." The lion turned his blond mane to his cub.

Sven had taken the next step in the lifelong practice of fly-fishing. The boy had watched Harry the fisherman artfully touch line to water, then pull fighting fillets from the pond's shallow depths. On that one-hundred-degree night, Sven used his Talon Mark IV graphite fly rod to tease a trout. Karl used his platinum mechanical hand to grasp the fish. Sven removed the hook from the trout's gasping gills. Karl released it back into the pond.

Across the pond's dilated ripples, C.J. and little Lucy patiently prayed for the red and white fishing bobber surfing the slight tsunami caused by young Sven's sweet success. The sparkle from both Karl and Sven's blue eyes drew C.J.'s attention away from the plastic bulb floating in the water to the handsome hope across the pond. Karl realized that C.J. cast a line out to him. In a flash, Karl and Sven came upon the two ladies. To Karl, C.J.'s eyes lit up the night with brilliance not unlike the aurora borealis striking the northern sky.

"Hi, Karl." Tears glazed over C.J.'s big zircon eyes.

"You look great, Capricious."

Only C.J.'s parents called her by her proper name. Now out of the distant past, her hero, her knight in shining armor stood before her and softly said her name with a warm tone on a hot night. She fell under his protective wing-so snug and so secure.

"It's nice to see you." Karl's spirit naturally rose to the moment. His voice deepened and calmed her. He turned to his son and said, "Why don't you help Lucy catch a fish?" The kids disappeared into the night-covered shoreline. Karl and C.J. disappeared into each other. Both were ten years old again.

"This pond isn't quite as nice as Farmers Pond." C.J. blushed as she spoke.

"No," he replied. The sound of his mellow tone drifted into her ears and into her soft soul. She felt his penetrating voice reverberate through her bones and melt her. Her flesh barely clung to her skeletal frame. "It's not quite Farmers

Pond, but it's all mine," he said. As he spoke, he spread his arms. The dichotomy of his muscular arm in contrast to the other man-made arm seared her consciousness. She tried not to look at it. Karl looked around and said, "The pond. Rainbow Rapids. The fish. It's all mine."

C.J. looked puzzled.

"I'm the architect and principle engineer of the river technology here. I designed it all. And I am the bioengineer at the fish farm. Our company built this place and stocks it with the finest genetically engineered fish in the entire world. They are the meatiest, healthiest, fiercest fighting fish anywhere."

"Oh, Karl. You were always so smart."

"And you were always so beautiful," Karl whispered.

C.J.'s face turned bright red. Karl reached for her with his left hand. He craved her touch. Reality revealed itself to C.J in the form of fear. She flinched. *No one could know.* What if Lucy saw them? C.J. felt so exposed-her emotions so open to the world. She felt raw and naked and scared.

"I'm sorry, Capricious."

"Karl, I can't. I'm married. I have a family."

"I know. I feel the same."

"What are we going to do?"

"We can be friends, can't we?"

"Yes. Yes. Friends. We can be friends." C.J. came to her senses.

"Friends?" Karl reached out his left hand again.

"Friends!" C.J. shook it in agreement and then said, "Tell me something interesting. Like you used to do at Farmers Pond."

Karl thought about it for a moment. "Hmmm. Something interesting, huh? I have something," he said.

C.J. loved the hum of his smooth-sounding voice.

"OK. Did you know that fish that live in salt water have more babies than fish that live in fresh water?"

"I didn't know that." C.J. smiled.

"Salt, you see, has for thousands of years been associated with fertility. The Romans described a man in love as *salax*-in a salted state. *Salax* is the origin of the word *salacious*. In the Pyrenees, couples going to church to be wed carried salt in their pockets in hopes that it would defend them against impotence." Karl inched closer to C.J. "In France the groom carried salt. In Germany the bride sprinkled it on her shoes. Celibate Egyptian holy men practiced abstinence from salt for fear it would excite unwanted desire." Karl inched closer and asked, "Shall I continue?" From his pocket he withdrew a small packet of salt and sprinkled its contents on her shoes.

"You carry salt around with you?" C.J. jumped back.

"I sprinkle it on my shoes!"

C.J. laughed. "You're crazy!"

"Now you tell me something." Karl stared into C.J.'s mind. "What have you been doing all these years?" he asked.

C.J. paused. Smiled. Her fear lifted and she beamed. "After we left Goodyear, we basically started over. My parents put me into another school. I graduated from high school, then went to college in San Diego."

"What did you study?" Karl asked.

"Business administration."

Karl smiled.

"Then I met Frank. Got married. Started a small public relations business. Had kids. Sold the business. The years went by. Nothing too exciting. I'm happy. I love my family. And here I am talking to you."

Karl looked at her. He secretly hoped that she was not happy. In that moment with her, he felt wonderful to be in her presence. To be talking to her. She continued with small talk. He pretended to listen. But could only wonder to himself if she read his note again. *Did she keep it? Had she been thinking about him? Maybe she threw it away for fear her husband would find it? Maybe she threw it away because she was disgusted by it?*

"Are you a partner in the Rainbow Rapids company?" C.J. caught his attention.

"Huh?" Karl had not been listening.

"Are you a partner in your business?"

"Uh, yes. Yes. Yes I am. I mean, I am going to be."

"What do you mean?"

"I mean they were supposed to make me a partner a while back, but never got around to it."

"What?"

"I am sure they are going to make good on our agreement."

"Doesn't sound good, Karl. Have you mentioned it to them?"

"Yes. But I am not going to keep bugging them. I am giving them a few more weeks to get around to it. They said they were nailing down the details of the firm's financial position and that they wanted to protect me from the debt."

"Sure. Of course. But keep asking them about it."

"So have you been thinking about me since Diamond's Department Store?" Karl changed the topic to a subject matter far more to his liking.

She turned flush red. Her heart raced.

"What about you, Karl? What happened to you after I left Goodyear?" She diverted attention away from the assault upon her fragile state.

"My story is basically the same as yours. School. Marriage. Kids. Work. I'm happy." Karl only wished to engage in discourse that stirred the precious emotion boiling in his gut. He wanted to discuss the note-the raw expression of torment that he cast upon his Capricious Harmony. Any other words proved meaningless to him.

"Tell me that you liked my note. That you loved my note. That you have been thinking about me!" he demanded.

"So where did you meet your wife, Karl?"

"Capricious! Tell me you loved my note!" Karl stepped toward C.J.

"How old are your kids?" C.J. took a step backward.

"I know you loved it! I know you did! You read it over and over again! You can't get it out of your head. You can't get me out of your head...your heart. You can't get me out of your heart!"

"Lucy!" C.J. turned toward the shore and ran away into the darkness.

Defeated, Karl walked toward the shore in the opposite direction. A glimmer of sparkling lights flashed across the pond's surface. The flashes blinded him. He heard a commanding voice. "Go to Nineveh. A great storm is coming," said the voice. And Karl came to his senses. God had spoken to Karl. *What had he done?* He thought of Nineveh, the mother of his two beautiful children.

* * *

A few months later in October, high gas prices, a large number of mortgage defaults, and structural deficiencies in the financial markets caused the stock market to plummet, money and credit markets to halt, and the world economy to fall into a severe recession.

AFTERMATH

OCTOBER 2008

T he 118-degree heat immediately penetrated the car. Both C.J. and Karl began to sweat. Terrified, she turned to him. They commiserated in the front seat of his parked car, contemplating the unknown. The uncharted nature of the journey upon which they embarked could not be ignored. In her mind, C.J. tried to focus on each moment. She tried to ignore her morbid imagination of the future- *the what if's.* Karl sensed her fear. Her nervous fidgeting scratched at him.

"Capricious, everything is going to be OK." He offered what little he could.

Frank's absence exasperated her anxiety. Her husband's conspicuous adherence to his career goals did not surprise her. It only reaffirmed her disappointment in him- that he would choose to go in to the office on this day. C.J. pictured him in his big corner office, leaning back in his high-backed cordovan leather and mahogany chair reading this month's edition of *High Net Worth* magazine. She recalled the current cover article: "Winning Strategies to

Compartmentalize Your Family and the Hindrance to Your Success."

Above C.J. and Karl, the sign on the office building read, "Desert Cancer Research Center." Karl expected to witness a leper colony inside. He envisioned frail and pale people cast aside, lurching around, waiting to greet Saint Peter. Despite his better sense, he reflected upon the possibility of cancer being contagious. *What if he caught it?*

"Come on, Capricious. We don't want to be late," he said.

Reluctantly, she dragged herself out of the passenger seat. Though a month had passed since her two surgeries, her entire upper body still felt sore. Though the surgery only cut from her breast a hunk of flesh measuring five centimeters in diameter, the pain equated to ten trucks smashing her body into the pavement. She rarely complained. Held her spirits as high as she could. Put on a brave face. But inside, she hurt. The constant electric shock sensation pulsating through her butchered lymph nodes reminded her that something was very wrong.

The next step, the next wave to endure, was the chemotherapy. Though she had tried to keep her condition private, her friends soon figured it out. They tried to be helpful, offering success stories of friends and relatives. Asking her if she had this symptom or that symptom-

encouraging her that those symptoms were to be expected. They offered secondhand advice to help her deal with the prospect of chemo. Unfortunately, none of it helped. Her fear persisted.

C.J.'s legs pedaled her toward the medical building's entrance. Always a gentleman, Karl reached for the door. In the direct sunlight, the door's handle was cloth covered to prevent unsuspecting people from scorching their fingers on its hot metal. Together the two crossed the threshold. Inside, the large number of cancer-inflicted patients struck Karl. He figured fifty people were in the waiting room. The place was full-standing room only. Karl immediately recognized that C.J. was the youngest person in that crowd. They all turned and stared at her and Karl. He figured they must have assumed that he and she were husband and wife. Karl secretly hoped that none of the crowd knew his wife, Nineveh. *How would he explain his presence there to his wife? But the cancer center seemed so far away from his daily life. Certainly no one would recognize him.*

Many of the male patients in the room covered their bald heads with hats: nautical captain's hats, veterans' hats, wide-brimmed fedora hats, Major League Baseball hats, and many more. The women wore loose-fitting humble wigs and brilliantly colored striped scarves. Karl admired one woman who refused to stand beneath such implements. She instead existed proudly in the world having not one hair sprouting through her wrinkled skin. Neither the lack of eyelashes, nor eyebrows, nor curls atop her head dared define that strong woman. Handsome King Karl winked at the bald queen. Her grey face turned a flush rose with her elderly beautiful blush. She smiled. The entire room smiled.

One of the friendly staff took C.J.'s name, insurance card, and payment. Another took her weight and another her vital statistics. A doctor wearing a maroon turban above his kind eyes warned her of manageable side effects caused by chemotherapy. He had founded the research center twenty years previously. With a trembling tone in her tender voice, C.J. asked, "Am I going to die?" Through his dark silver beard, he replied, "You're going to live to see your grandchildren, my dear young lady." C.J. cried. Karl declared the doctor a saint. Everyone in the center boasted about life.

After consulting with the oncologist, C.J. and Karl walked timidly past the American Cancer Society room in which patients could select from a collection of donated wigs and scarves. They came into the chemo room-a large room lined with rows of comfortably cushioned reclining chairs in which patients dozed while nurses flooded them intravenously with cocktails comprised of tough drugs, radiated blood transfusions, and much more. From elevated clear plastic bags hanging from rolling stands, liquids dripped lovingly and sometimes painfully into the thirsty veins waiting below.

In one of those chairs, C.J. sat. Karl watched as a serious nurse with a friendly voice and a floral-patterned loose-fitting shirt poked C.J. with a needle. The nurse fidgeted with a plastic valve located on the line from a bag above leading down into C.J. *Clear liquid dripped into his Capricious Harmony.* Karl could see that the liquid felt cold inside her body. She shivered. He covered her with a warm blanket.

"Karl, I almost forgot to give this to you," said C.J. She handed Karl a sheet of paper, closed her big eyes, and fell asleep.

"The medicine does that," said the nurse. Karl read C.J.'s letter:

October 20, 2008

Dear Richard Sully,

The purpose of this letter is to summarize the events that have occurred since June 1, 2000, as they relate to our contract.

On June 1, 2000, Rainbow Rapids River Technology and Fish Farm Company ("Rainbow Rapids") and I, Karl Hoogeveen, agreed to a mutually beneficial contract that began on July 1, 2000 (See enclosed). According to the terms of the agreement, I was to progress from being a third-party contractor to Rainbow Rapids, through being a Rainbow Rapids employee, then on to becoming a member of the company, Rainbow Rapids, with an increasing share of ownership according to a schedule of milestones to which both Rainbow Rapids and I consented. As of October 20, 2008, Rainbow Rapids has failed to perform its contractual obligation. For this cause, I am terminating my employment with Rainbow Rapids.

After I acted in good faith, met my deliverables according to the contract terms in addition to meeting other additional goals outside of the original priorities (to the extent that Rainbow Rapids annually rewarded my outstanding achievements and good standing with a 10% salary increase) and after I made repeated inquiries to Rainbow Rapids regarding the disposition of Rainbow Rapids' progress to meet its obligation, Rainbow Rapids took no action to fulfill the terms of the contract.

At this time, I am calling a meeting to be held on October 23, 2008, between the board of directors, you, and me. The purpose of the meeting is to ensure full disclosure of the contents of this letter and my financial ownership position in Rainbow Rapids prior to any sale or change in control of Rainbow Rapids.

Kind regards,

Karl Hoogeven

C.J. had written the letter on his behalf. Karl admired her strong business sense. Not caring about his employment situation, he paused his thoughts and looked around the "Chemo Café." In a heavy accent, an Italian man having an age not less than one hundred years flirted with three pretty nurses and another quite ugly one by the measure of her prickly demeanor. She was not at all nice. She emitted a lot of fire and a bit of ice.

Then Karl saw a tiny but tenacious ladybird walk under the wing of a giant eagle-the woman's husband. Tastefully dotted with candy apple red lipstick and nail polish, the woman held him up and pushed him onward with all her little might. Her dainty knees wobbled. The weight of her husband's arm around her neck and shoulders forced her face to look down. She watched her hand-painted cowgirl boots inch forward beneath her. Her silver and turquoise jewelry jingled as she moved. She also saw her husband's tan ostrich skin boots shuffle as he barely found the strength to drag them along. Three nurses ran to her aid. They huddled around him as if he had just come in from days in the dust-driving cattle across the Arizona high country. A cowboy he was. His withered ranch clothes gave him authenticity. Karl imagined that the man owned a ranch that had been in the family for generations. The man appeared rich but rugged. He had obviously thinned. His thick bones accounted for the majority of his weight. The man and the small crowd around him tottered past Karl into a small side room where the medical staff could administer the chemotherapy to him while he lay down on a bed. He had not the strength to even sit. Karl hoped that C.J. would never end up in that room.

Over the course of eighteen weeks, C.J. marched through the regiment with Karl at her side. The two learned to arrive early to get a good seat. The staff came to know them quite well. Karl eavesdropped on many discussions at the "Café." The topics included cancer-interrupted vacation plans, breast reductions, augmentations, daughters who died, and daughters who lived; of being under the knife and enduring a Christmas through chemo; of living ten years or more. Karl kept stonefaced with an occasional warm smile. He felt helpless while struggling to be helpful. C.J. merely appreciated his presence. She had not had to endure the ordeal alone.

After each session while C.J.'s kid's were with their grandmother, Karl took C.J. to his mother's home close by the Chemo Café. There, C.J. slept and found comfort beneath his mother Rebekka's soft caring touch across her feverish forehead. C.J. never blamed Karl's mother for Bram's actions thirty years previous. And Karl's mother found taking care of Capricious soothing. His mother wanted to give back to Capricious what little she could. At one point after Capricious's hair began to fall out in huge clumps, Rebekka shaved all three of their heads in solidarity. Capricious was not alone.

* * *

Karl was late. He had been held up at work. One of the pumps at Rainbow Rapids had failed. Behind the wheel of his car he sped into the Chemo Café's parking lot. He slammed the brakes and abruptly parked the car. The sight of flashing red and blue lights atop a bright red fire department paramedic truck with big heavy-duty tires and a box-shaped white ambulance with small tires alarmed Karl. He wondered which of his friends inside was in peril. Was it kind Peter with lymphoma, or sweet Sarah with the brain tumor? Could it have homeless Henry with the prostate problem? Maybe it was Mary with lung cancer.

Karl jumped out of the car and ran past the emergency vehicles. He heard the idling engines purr, and he tasted diesel exhaust. The flashing lights reflected up on the medical building's wall. He hurried through the front door. The staff beeped him through the locked entrance leading into the chemo room. He immediately saw the lemon-colored steel ambulance gurney on the opposite side of the room. Two brawny handsome firemen paramedics stood calmly in blue cotton tee shirts and pants. Huge white letters across their backs read "CFD." Two cute nurses recited in high-pitched monotones vital statistics.

The paramedic's black steel and rubber walkie-talkies screeched and crackled. Karl looked down each row of reclining chemo chairs for his Capricious. But Capricious was not there. He looked again. He saw Peter, Sarah, and Henry. Then Mary, who pointed to the side room. Oh no! Not the side room! Karl rushed past his hairless friends. Two other paramedics, a doctor, and two nurses crammed the small space in the side room. Karl could not see who was lying on the bed. Who was it? He wanted it to be him instead. Through the crowd he caught sight of her. Capricious looked at him in peace and smiled. Blood dripped from the inside of her ear and from her nose.

"You'll have to wait out here," the nurse said and closed the door.

"No! No! Capricious!" Karl screamed.

In the middle of the night, he woke. His fright had only been a terrible dream.

* * *

Readied for battle, Karl read once more through his letter of resignation authored by his companion, counsel, and secret lethal weapon, Capricious. Since he was a kindhearted man, such confrontations eluded his liking. Argumentative dialogue and quick natured debate displeased him. But he knew that the deed must be done. The situation necessitated action. He feared not.

At the Rainbow Rapids company's Phoenix office, he waited outside Richard Sully's corner office. Karl then decided that war would be waged best with an empty bladder and a clean scent upon his person.

Inside the restroom, a voice echoed against the fancy marble and tile walls and floors. "Karl, is that you?" said the voice. Karl recognized the voice coming from within a foul-smelling stall.

"Yes. It's me." Karl's shoulders shrank.

Richard Sully had caught him in the bathroom once again. The CEO and president of Rainbow Rapids had a habit of holding impromptu meetings in the washroom.

"We gotta' do somethin' about this hemorrhage! The company is bleeding! Five cancelled projects!" Richard Sully's voice bounced around the walls.

"So what was it that you wanted to discuss?"

Karl slid the letter under the stall. Silence ensued. Gases *ad nauseam* persisted from Richard Sully's porcelain pot. Karl knew according to the art of negotiating that the first person to speak always loses. Karl held strong. Said nothing and let the dead calm set and the silence settle. The letter said it all. He heard Richard Sully exhale as he flipped the pages of the letter.

"Go home, Karl. I'll call you tomorrow."

Three days later Karl sat in his home at his desk calculating his next move. With Capricious's help, Karl effectively blocked the sale of Rainbow Rapids. Capricious had advised Karl that the owners of the company would be held personally liable if the company had any claims against it. Karl had a legitimate claim to shares of the company.

"Daddy, you've messed up my desk again!" little Karla scolded him.

Karl had shared his desk with his daughter for quite some time. Slowly her crayons and fixtures had overtaken Karl's things atop his desk. Her important purple activity planner filled with birthday party dates, her list of Internet passwords, her charm bracelets, her bubblegum, her play cell phone, and her other important items had overtaken the desk. She relegated Karl and his belongings to the far outer corner. As his papers moved inward toward the center, she declared a penalty.

Just then, the phone rang.

"Karl!" said the voice on the other end of the line.

"Yes."

"It's Bob." Bob worked up north at the fishery with Karl. "I just found out. Have you heard?"

"Heard what?"

"Ummm. Rainbow Rapids. Rainbow Rapids declared bankruptcy. It's all over."

* * *

About a year later in 2009, C.J. and her husband, Frank, arrived at the medical office five minutes before her appointment at ten thirty. The thermometer this late summer morning read one hundred and four. By late summer everybody who lived in the valley of the Sun grew tired of the heat.

Frank sweated, but not just from the temperature outside. He worried about medical insurance and his employment situation. During the recession Frank lost his job. His win-loss management style finally caught with him when things got tight at the company. He had won too many personal battles at work with the wrong people. In the end the second placers pushed him out of the company and onto the street.

The knot in Frank's stomach proved chronic. He never got used to these visits-however infrequently he chose to go. Everybody kept telling him that the caregiver took much of the pain, the mental pain—the anguish and worry. Essentially, though, Frank thought otherwise. He knew that he was not much of a caregiver. He could only imagine how she felt. It depressed him too much to think about it. He knew she relied upon him to be strong and at times, he felt a little guilty about not being there for her during the treatment.

During conversations with doctors in which Frank was present, C.J. would look at Frank to measure his reaction to the doctors' words. Despite her knowing that beneath his tough exterior, he proved weak, she still needed him to help her. He could only resort to never showing any emotion. He figured it was best to be just a tough rock upon which C.J. could rely. C.J. concluded Frank was emotionally detached, distant, and uncaring. She wanted him to be strong, while at the same time being compassionate and understanding. He never measured up to her hope.

The sign on the door read "Dr. Eldon Blackburn Board of American Association of Breast Surgeons." Dr. Blackburn once told Frank and C.J. that he had descended from US Marshal Leslie Blackburn from Tombstone, Arizona, and that Marshal Blackburn had once put into custody Doc Holiday during the early 1850s.

Frank had noticed the doctor backing a new super-duty pickup truck into his covered and shaded parking spot. He had also noticed the classic rifle mounted on the truck's back window. Frank wondered why in such an empty office parking lot the doctor paid for the "Reserved: Surgeon" stencil on the cement parking stop.

C.J. walked up to the administrative desk, and Frank took a seat to listen to the piped-in country music and flip through the women's magazines neatly stacked on the coffee table. She signed in after greeting the office assistant at the desk. C.J. admired her large bosom. Frank had once joked that the doc had a fascination with big breasts, as all the women who worked in the office shared that common trait. Frank looked at C.J's shapely calves. During the past year, her body had been through so much, and her shape had lost its vigor. Even her mind had become dull. In the past she never missed a detail—never made a mistake. But after about a year of treatment, the little things escaped C.J.'s awareness. Her calves seemed about the only part of her body left intact.

And then Frank looked at the wall just beyond her legs where she stood. It appeared that someone had kicked a hole through the white plaster. Frank imagined an irate husband losing control at the desk. *And why not?* Frank could easily sympathize with an upset spouse. He remembered after C.J.'s second surgery to "widen the margins," Dr. Blackburn left Frank waiting in the consultation room. The doctor had left the hospital not bothering to inform Frank of C.J.'s condition and of the surgery. And the doctor had lied about the number of malignant sentinel lymph nodes he had removed. Dr. Blackburn informed Frank of removing two; but later Frank read from the medical records that he had removed eight—"two banks of four." Frank figured the doctor had spared him the angst.

After that experience Frank stopped asking questions and reading the medical reports. He resolved not to know too much. He was not a medical doctor. Her serious condition required acute and rapid care. *Was he going to question the course of action? The doctor had thirty-five years of experience.*

"Capricious." The medical assistant called her into the examination room.

As Frank and C.J. walked, Frank permitted Margaret, the medical assistant, and C.J. to walk before him. Margaret looked like she should have worked at a truck stop. She chewed gum and wore heavily painted cosmetics. She eyed C.J. from the top of C.J.'s head down to the tip of her toe. Frank remembered Margaret had done the same head-to-toe analysis during their first visit a year ago. At that time Frank had been accustomed to passersby gawking at his stunning wife. Frank figured Margaret recognized the dramatic change. He saw pity in Margaret's countenance. He tried not to think about all the drama and instead thought about C.J.'s survival. She was alive. The kids still had their young mother. Frank's eyes watered. He held back the tears.

"Room three in there," said Margaret. "Your hair looks nice."

C.J. no longer wore the wig. The nurses had warned that when her hair grew back, it might come back a different color. Frank believed God had blessed C.J. not only with her life, but also with her beautiful brown locks sprouting once again without change. He believed Margaret spoke from the heart.

Margaret left the room. And they waited. And waited. And waited. Frank hated waiting for doctors. Rarely did they arrive on time. He could hear C.J.'s heart beating rapidly with fear. She sweated profusely under the arms. She smelled badly, and the odor filled the room. Then Dr. Blackburn entered.

"Hello," he said with cheer. "Sorry I'm late. Having a bad day." He raised his two arms and displayed casts on both arms and around his thumbs.

"Both thumbs broken this morning. Just got these damn things put on. I won't be doing any cutting for a few weeks."

Frank's jaw dropped. He thought of the irate husband.

The doctor wore his blue surgery room garb and a black surgery hat with skull and crossbones on it. Normally during office visits, he wore dress slacks, a button-down shirt, and a pair of black boots.

"Did you bring the records I asked you to?" The doctor looked sternly at Frank.

"Yes. I gave them to Margaret."

"Well? Where the hell are they?"

"Uh. She has the CD."

"The CD? How the hell am I supposed to read a CD? You know how much information they put on those CDs? Did you think about that? How I am supposed to muddle through all of that crap? Did you ask Margaret to print what I need?"

"Uh. I...Perhaps the records are in the manila envelope she left on the examination table?"

"Oh! Here they are. Let's see what we are dealin' with." Dr. Blackburn began licking the tip of his cast-wrapped thumb and separating sheets of medical reports.

"Hmm. OK. I see. Mmm."

C.J.'s eyes and the stains under her arms widened.

Then the doctor's cell phone rang.

"Uh, hang on. I gotta take this."

He struggled to retrieve the phone from his pocket. The casts proved burdensome. But after great effort, he flipped it open to answer it.

"Yea, it's me."

The phone mumbled with a voice on the other end.

"No. I haven't given any order. What's it say in the computer?"

The phone mumbled.

"There's nothin' in the computer?"

The phone mumbled.

"You sure?"

The phone mumbled.

"Well. Just ship 'er down to the morgue."

The phone mumbled.

"What do you mean you can't do it without an order?"

The phone mumbled.

"No. No. Don't put my name on the order. Hmm. What's the family want to do?"

The phone mumbled.

"Well, then, call the family. Find out what they want to do. And don't put my name on anything."

The phone mumbled. Then the doctor closed the phone.

"Bad breast day!" he exclaimed.

C.J.'s eyes widened even further.

"OK. So let's see about you and what we're dealin' with. We had the sentinel biopsy and lumpectomy. Then the wide excision. Then over at the cancer center, eighteen weeks of chemotherapy. And you just finished the year of hormone treatment, correct?"

"Yes." C.J. bowed her head and looked down at the expensive Arizona slate tile.

C.J. and Karl had spent so many hours there. They both had come to believe the center was full of compassionate saints. Everyone there cared. And the founder of the center, Dr. Sengupta the oncologist, was the only doctor to tell C.J. that she would live to see her grandchildren. All the others took a defensive stance. None of them gave C.J. any hope. Just told her to cross her fingers. Dr. Blackburn had complained to C.J. that Dr. Sengupta had soft hands and a weak handshake. C.J. on the contrary, appreciated Dr. Sengupta's kindness.

"Right. You had thirty-three radiation treatments, and now you are on the daily chemo pill?"

"Yes."

"And you just had an MRI guided biopsy, mammogram, and sonogram?"

"Yes. And the PET scan."

"I don't see that here. Lemme look." He flipped through the pages.

"Here it is. Yes. Did you get the results of the MRI?"

"No."

"Well. It says here in the report that it's not positive. So that's good."

"What do you mean not positive?"

"The result is indeterminate. That means they don't know what they are seeing. Which is not bad. So that's good."

"So now what?" she asked. C.J was not encouraged. She looked at Frank for his reaction. He sat cold-faced.

"So now we keep an eye on you every few months. For today let's have a look-see at your breast."

C.J. grabbed the pink paper examination vest.

"There's no need for that thing."

The doctor asked her to sit on the examination table. He reached down her shirt and into her bra to examine his work.

"Good. It's nice 'n supple. It's healing. You using the vitamin E lotion?"

"Yes."

Neither C.J. nor Frank minded him reaching into her blouse. They were beyond formality. He had cut into her twice and saved her life. For that they were eternally grateful to him. Despite his gruff ways, both C.J. and Frank loved Dr. Blackburn. To them, he too was a saint.

Fresh Kill

December 2009

The light went on—the "Check Engine" light. C.J. pulled over immediately. She remembered that her daddy had told her never to drive with "the light on."

"Oh, dear."

She thought momentarily about calling her husband, but then decided against it. Frank would most likely add to the problem. He would be annoyed that she had interrupted him listening to off-season baseball AM radio. He would ask odd questions that she could not answer. Inevitably they would fight. She had been looking forward to a quiet day at the mall to shop for inexpensive Christmas gifts for the kids. Fighting with Frank was not in her plan.

C.J. then considered taking her SUV over to the dealership. But she knew the dealership was overpriced. *Those guys would take her to the cleaners and rob her blind.* And Frank had been laid off. They had no income. Against her advice over the years, he had spent a large portion of their savings and income on unneeded stuff: an oversized house, fancy cars, lavish vacations, and expensive toys—the Jet Skis, the boat, the RV...And the money she earned from selling her business had been tied up (frozen by a judge that sat on a Maricopa County Court bench) in a frivolous copyright dispute. C.J. could not afford to take the SUV to the dealership.

Her mind raced. She flipped through a small stack of business cards she kept in her designer purse. The rhythm of her pulse caught her attention. It reminded her of being in the doctor's office waiting for the results of biopsies and MRIs. She put that memory out of her thought.

"Ah. Here it is." She smiled. She held up high a black-and-white checkered card that read "Queen Creek Quality Car Care." One of the landscape crew that used to tend to their lawn prior to Frank's layoff recommended the garage to her. The shop was located just passed historic downtown Queen Creek over near Old Hunt Highway (named after Arizona's first governor) beyond where the city had been building things up. She started the engine and drove toward the garage.

Originally a farming community, Queen Creek had recently been transformed with huge tracts of new homes, large brand-name department stores, and big corporate bank branches. Amid the new construction, the town trustees took great care to preserve its heritage and several historic sites. C.J.'s drive took her past a World War II prisoner of war camp in which the United States military kept captured German soldiers. After the war ended and the camp closed, many of the German soldiers stayed and settled in the Queen Creek farming community. She continued on past the Desert Wells Stage Stop. The Arizona Stage Company, founded in 1868, established the stop to provide water and shade for weary desert travelers coming from Florence.

She enjoyed the ambiance of the old charm preserved by the surrounding modern amenities. However, ever since the recent economic bust, all of the new construction had ceased—halting the town's vision from coming to life. She passed several unfinished neighborhoods and abandoned home building sites. Rancho Opulente was bad enough with all of its awful bright-yellow sheriff foreclosure stickers on so many of its homes and overgrown weeds taking over several of the yards. The desert vegetation appeared to be reclaiming Rancho Opulente.

The old town section through which C.J. drove was even worse. Several of the builders had gone out of business. She felt sorry for the people who had bought homes over there. She imagined living in a neighborhood with only two or three finished homes surrounded by dozens of empty lots and withering frames. *Ugh. And they had bought in 2008 when home prices peaked just before the housing market crashed.*

Beyond the old town just past Hunt Highway, the newly paved road upon which she drove transitioned into a decaying pothole-filled street. Years of seasonal hundred-and-fifteen-plus-degree weather had softened the street's tar. Farm machines and light traffic molded its shape to conform to the rough landscape beneath. About a half mile down the road, she saw a crooked and rusty "Quality Care" sign hanging on one nail. Behind it Gold Mine Mountain cast its metallurgical legacy.

Then her car died. The engine froze, and everything went eerily silent. C.J. panicked.

"No. Please. No."

Her heart tapped at the inside of her chest once again, but she found comfort in the fact that she could see the auto care garage just a short distance ahead. Determined, she resolved to lock up the car and march in her high heels to the auto mechanic.

She stepped out of the car and immediately smelled the scent of farming. It reminded her of her childhood; of the day she and Karl escaped to Farmers Pond. She loved that rich, rank scent. A big malachite-green tractor pulling a dairy cow feed spreader approached on the opposite side of the winding road. A young dapper Chilean man drove the machine. He stopped it just as he neared C.J.

"*Hola, senora. Buen Dia,*" said the man. He smiled and stepped off the tractor. His stunning good looks made an impression upon C.J. He did not appear poor and destitute. Rather, his pants were clean and pressed to a pair of perfect creases. He wore an expensive-looking traditional *chupalla* horseman's hat and no shirt.

"May I offer you a ride, *senora?*"

"No. No, thank you."

"I'm not going to hurt you, *senora.*"

"No. No, thank you. It's just up here. Thank you, no."

"OK. *Si tu dices.*"

He boarded his cactus-colored monster and continued on his way. C.J. turned to see a sticker on the back of the dairy cow feeder that read, "Drink Milk!" She chuckled and walked on. Her dainty steps along soft tar and Valley of the Sun soil tarnished her pedicure and ruined her shoes. Then she arrived at Hell's Gate.

The place had not changed since its first day of business in 1955. Popular in its day, black and white vinyl covered the floor. A calendar with a Tempest Storm pinup hung behind the space-age design aluminum sales counter. Time, spilled soda pop, and monsoon humidity had rusted its seams. Tetanus loomed beneath the countertop.

C.J. stepped up and placed her imported Parisian purse next to the mechanically operated, thick, metal cash register.

"May I help you?"

A large bald man with a grey mechanic's shirt and a blood-red-lettered name patch that read "Bob" stood looking down at her purse. He spoke softly and did not dare look her in the eye. While he spoke, he turned his head to hide the bad side of his face. C.J. caught a glimpse of the permanent gash and scarring embedded into his expressions. It appeared to her that someone had beaten him with a tire iron or similar instrument. She took pity upon the gentle giant and smiled. Her warmth came into his person. She soothed him.

"Um, yes. You can." C.J. spoke softly in turn. "My car died."

"OK. Where is it?"

"Just down the road about a half mile."

"OK. I'll send the wrecker to tow it in."

C.J. smiled and winked at him. He blushed and began filling out paperwork.

"Will you be waiting here? Or will someone be picking you up?" he asked.

"I'll wait," she said.

"Have a seat. We'll call you when we know what's wrong," Bob said. "It'll be a while. Make yourself comfortable. There's coffee over there." He pointed to the coffee machine in the corner of the room.

As C.J. walked to the waiting area, she looked at the wulfenite-yellow glass coffee pitcher. Several fungus varieties grew around its rim. And then she rifled through hot rod magazines decorated with bikini-clad teens. The entire establishment smelled of oil and grease.

Thirty minutes later she saw through the dirty window in the waiting room the tow truck pulling her SUV around to the back of that store. An hour after her car entered the lot, a tall, thin, handsome young man called her up to the counter.

His broad smile, sparkling white teeth, and profound eyes welcomed her.

"I'm Nathanial," he said.

"Hi."

"I have some good news and some bad news."

"Hmm." C.J. sighed with worry.

"We put fresh motor oil in the car. It started. But the bad news is that a loud rattling noise is coming from the engine. We've removed several of the parts, and we're digging down...But we're just not sure what the rattling is. It sounds very deep and very internal."

And very expensive, she thought. "What should I do?" C.J. felt helpless.

"Well, we'd like to keep the car overnight. We can call you tomorrow afternoon, if you like."

"OK." She turned pale.

"Shall I call you a taxi?" he asked.

She nodded.

That night in the early evening while Frank slept, C.J. called the landscape worker that had given her the Queen Creek Quality Auto Care business card. He had written his number on the back of the card in case she ever needed him for side jobs. Frank had not noticed her SUV missing from their empty five-car garage. C.J. had sold three of the cars, leaving only her SUV and his sports car. He was still making payments on his car. Hers was paid off. On the phone she inquired about a rattling noise and learned from him that it may be the timing chain.

"Shouldn't be too expensive," he said.

Relieved, she hung up the phone and began reviewing their finances. She calculated that they had enough money to live for about four months before they would have to think about abandoning the house. She thought about settling the lawsuit. To be done with it. To salvage what little money would be left after the lawyer's fees. She thought about looking for work.

The next day she found Frank castrated on the couch again. He had not shaved for days. Smelled of alcohol—he had switched from beer to cheap sour mash. The house was a mess. Then the phone rang.

"Hello." C.J. grabbed the wireless receiver and stepped outside, away from Frank's ability to eavesdrop upon her conversation.

"Hello, Ms. Harmony, this is Nathanial from Quality Auto Care." He spoke smoothly, with a reassuring tone of voice.

"How does it look?"

"Well, the timing assembly is shot. We also dropped the oil pan and pulled off the piston valve covers. Both are sparkling!"

"Fantastic. That sounds great!"

"No ma'am. That's bad."

"I don't understand. Sparkling sounds good," she concluded.

"If we were speaking about cosmetics and nail polish, then yes, sparkling is pretty. But when we refer to oil pans and pistons, sparkling is bad. It means something is grinding, and the shavings are disbursing throughout the engine."

"What are you saying?"

"I am saying that you have a decision to make."

"What do you mean?"

"Well. I am saying that things are not good."

"I'm confused. Why don't I come down there? I would like to see what you are talking about."

"Sure. No problem. We would love to see your pretty smile."

C.J. knew nothing about engines. She felt vulnerable and hated the sensation. *How would she prevent them from taking advantage of her?* He would show her the problem. She would not understand. Her family could not afford this situation. And Frank would get the upper hand. He would have reason to blame her—to point the finger at her. The argument would change from him being lazy on the couch to her screwing up. C.J. determined that she would somehow find a way out of this jam.

Arriving at the auto shop by bicycle, C.J. used all of her strong sensibilities to squash her fear. By that December she had regained her strength after her cancer treatment and thus appreciated the enjoyable bike ride through mild seventy-degree climate. Winters in Phoenix were absolutely beautiful. Wearing jeans, light makeup, and tennis shoes, she entered the building. She stood tall and confident. Then she looked slick Nathaniel straight in the eye. Did not smile. She was prepared to do battle.

Nathaniel led C.J. through the shop and out to the backyard. The garage was not a garage at all. She was surprised to discover that they worked on cars out in the open. And the mechanics randomly arranged the cars rather than in ordered lines. It appeared to her to be inefficient and unorganized. Out toward the edge of the property lot, she saw her light-grey SUV—absent its hood, with disassembled parts strewn around it. She felt like she was at the hospital visiting a sick family member.

As Nathaniel paraded C.J. through the lot, all the mechanics paused their tasks to gawk at her vigor and shape, which had returned to her. She could feel her face turn red. To affirm his dominance over her, he tried to walk quickly ahead of her. She refused to be his prey and kept pace with him by his side.

The two came upon her car. It rested on its front wheel rotors and pointed down into the earth. A group of four other mechanics circled Nathaniel and C.J. to observe the proceedings. Nathaniel bent down and began his demonstration. He showed her the oil pan, the piston valve covers, and the timing assembly. She could see the sparkling shavings in the cool sunlight.

"What's your recommendation?" she asked.

"We have several options. You could buy a new car. You could replace the engine. Or you can have the engine rebuilt." Nathaniel looked her in the eye.

She stood among the circle of five and froze. Regained her composure.

"I'll have to think about it. I don't think I want to buy a new car."

"Rebuilding the engine may not be a good idea either. The labor itself will be the same as if you replace the engine."

"So you're recommending that I replace the engine."

"Yes," he said and looked at her warmly. "We replace engines all the time. In fact, we just replaced one last week. It's really no big deal."

C.J. sensed he was lying. *How often does a shop replace an entire engine?*

"How much is an engine?" asked C.J.

"Well, I just happened to have called our parts supplier. We found a used one with only thirty thousand miles on it. I spoke to our manager, and we can install it for you for a total price of thirty-eight hundred dollars."

C.J. stood expressionless.

"Now I know this is a big decision," he said, trying to reassure her.

"I'll need some time to think about it."

"Sure. Take all the time you need. Do you have any other questions?"

"I think so. Ummm. So, 'used engine' means that you get this engine from a junkyard?"

"Yes. That's right."

"How do I know the condition of the engine?"

"Of course, we have a close relationship with this supplier. We've done business with him for many, many years. If he says it's in good condition, then it's in good condition. Of course, we'll warranty the engine and the labor."

"What's the warranty period?"

"Ninety days."

"Can I see the car at the junkyard?"

"You don't need to see the car," instructed Nathaniel. Insulted, he looked down at C.J. The circle of four mechanics looked at her too. Nobody smiled. She felt like she was about to be brutally attacked by them.

"You can see the engine when it's delivered here prior to installation."

C.J. did not understand why she could not inspect the engine at the junkyard.

"I am going to have to sleep on it. Why don't we talk again tomorrow?" she said timidly. Her hands shook nervously by her side. Her knees twitched. She hoped that Lucifer and his circle of mates did not see her quaking.

"Absolutely," said Nathaniel. He motioned to Half-Faced Bob to escort her out of the yard. As C.J. and Bob walked, she sensed Nathaniel staring at Bob.

"Do you know anything about the engine, Bob?" C.J. said with a flirtatious ring and a wink. Bob looked at the dirt. He too knew Nathaniel was watching.

"Nah. I dunno. I don't remember what the junkyard supplier said."

"You were the one who called for the engine?"

"Yes."

"What was the name of the junkyard?"

"Valley of the Sun Auto Parts." Bob looked over his shoulder at Nathaniel.

Then C.J. proceeded home. As before, she enjoyed riding her bike. During those days a healthy diet and exercise helped her manage the side effects of the daily pills of chemo the doctor prescribed. She enjoyed being outside and feeling the wind blowing through her hair. Since during summer days the dust storms made riding uncomfortable and other days the heat was unbearable, she cherished the good weather during spring and winter.

Upon her arrival home and in the privacy of her finished basement game room, C.J. dialed her cell phone.

"Valley of the Sun Auto Parts. Byrne speaking. How may I help you?" The man on the other end of the phone coughed a smoker's hack.

C.J. merely asked if they had in stock an engine for her SUV make and model.

"Just one moment, ma'am."

She heard him typing the computer. And then he exclaimed, "Fresh kill! Just got this one in a few days ago! I can let you have it for fifteen hundred dollars."

"How many miles does it have on it?"

"Only ninety-five thousand miles. Plenty of life left in it."

C.J.'s heart sank. Nathaniel had told her it had thirty thousand miles on it.

"And that's the only one you have for this SUV?"

"That's right, ma'am. They don't grow these things on trees. I doubt you'll find another one in Arizona."

"Well, OK. I'll have to think about it."

Out of curiosity C.J. browsed the Valley of the Sun's Internet website. On the company homepage, a photo of the company's entrance to the junkyard greeted each guest to the website. The image immediately struck her. She recognized the deep fuchsia Nova Zembla Rhododendron growing around the establishment's sign in Goodyear, where she grew up. Those non-indigenous plants had been there for at least thirty years. She remembered Karl and herself playing in that junkyard as kids.

HURRICANE

OCTOBER 1974

Young Capricious and little Karl ventured out together on another journey of fun. On that Saturday morning, Karl had led Capricious once again through Farmer Barlow's cotton field, past Farmer McNeal's dairy farm, and beyond Farmers Pond. He took her to explore the wondrous world within the walls around the Valley of the Sun Auto Parts junkyard.

The two snuck by the Nova Zembla Rhododendron and past the front office. They proceeded to the auto graveyard out back. To Capricious the maze of dead cars littered about provoked her imagination. She postulated the circumstances of each car's demise and of each family riding within. She wondered if anyone had lost his or her life. Such thoughts left her feeling empty and a bit sad.

Each automobile kept secret its history. To one side Capricious saw an amethyst purple pile of metal twisted around itself. She knew no one could have survived such a crash. It looked like a family sedan. She hoped no children had been in that car. To another side she pointed to an olivine-green car, crunched and crinkled. Karl threw a large rock at its windshield. The glass shattered with a thud, then a dangerous splash. An array of sharp glitter lit up the world, reflecting the high noon sun. Capricious feared his pitch drew attention from the inhabitants at the office. But it did not.

Off to the corner of the lot, situated in a spot all to itself, a psychedelic van moaned soulfully. The ghosts within it called to Capricious and Karl. Beckoned them to come forward. It appeared strangely familiar, but unrecognizable. It looked like a piece of multicolored paper crumbled into a ball. In silence they answered the ghosts' call and moved closer to it.

The night before, Friday night, the night of the big rivalry football game between Goodyear High School and the Phoenix Jesuit College Preparatory Academy, Billy the Bully's older sister, Christine, drove up to Karl's house to pick up Bram. Christine was the same girl who habitually brought Bram meals at his whim—the same girl who had served him dinner the day that Thunder, the Border Patrol canine, shook the neighborhood. Once again Capricious's sixteen-year-old sister, Lucille, hid in the back of the psychedelic van. Twenty-two-year-old Bram descended from his apartment above the garage and darted into the van's passenger seat next to Billy the Bully's sister, Christine. She drove "The Rock" love trio to the game.

As honor-roll students filled with Goodyear High pride, both Lucy and Christine had truthfully told their parents they would be going to the big game to cheer on the fierce Fighting Falcons.

"Do you two know Marsha Mathews?" Bram asked with an innocent high tone of voice.

Of course they knew Marsha. Everyone knew Marsha and the Mathews family. Her father owned the defense contractor company for which Capricious and Lucy's father, Don, worked. The Mathews family lived north of Phoenix in Paradise Valley. During the early-and mid-twentieth century, wealthy captains of industry and commerce built their mansions in Phoenix near the plush resorts of the day. Later in the century as Phoenix grew and diversified, the wealthy settled to the north in Paradise Valley.

Bram easily dissuaded the kids away from the football game. Driving through Phoenix, the trio passed the historic Wrigley Mansion built by the chewing gum tycoon, William Wrigley Jr. Its 1932 architecture, influenced by Spanish and Mediterranean style, stood as an icon of the period's elegant opulence that overlooked the vast Sonoran Desert and the beautiful city within.

Further north at a slightly higher elevation, they entered the town of Paradise Valley. The town founders' mission was to preserve the essence and lifestyle of the original community against the rapid Phoenix city expansion threatening it from down below. Those values included limited government that maintained its residential quiet character, its unobstructed views overlooking the valley, and its commitment to environmental preservation.

No noise. No light. They wanted to see the stars at night. Minimum lot size and home square footage requirements meant no poor. Everybody knew that the poor were the purveyors of unwanted noise and distracting light.

The teens and Bram drove by the private homes of the Maytag family and Senator Gerry Holdwater. On the Maytag property, they saw exotic animals roaming about: camels, zebra, and elephants. Finally beneath the backdrop of Mummy Mountain, they arrived at Mathews Mansion.

The mansion was a knockoff inspired by Paolo Selari's (a student of Frank Lloyd Wright) arcology movement at Arcostanti, Arizona—an experimental community of earthen solar-powered buildings and residences that merged together the concepts of architecture with ecology. True to Frank Lloyd Wright's school of thought, the Mathews mansion's distinctive geometric purity and organic lines blended into the earth. The interior's use of coordinated space and utilitarian fixtures further exemplified Frank Lloyd Wright's influence.

Unfortunately, the color combinations within the house would have made Mr. Wright turn in his grave. Mrs. Mathews described the inside of the house as "groovy." For instance, the living room featured wallpaper having various shades of lime green figure eights complemented with bright orange shag carpet. As the trio entered the house, then full of partygoers, they concurred with Mrs. Mathews and declared, "Groovy!"

Neither Christine nor Lucy had ever been in a home as large as the Mathews house. Both marveled at the vast number of rooms and expensive new 1970s postmodern furniture. Teenage Marsha had hired a popular local rock-and-roll cover band to play at the party. Large ice-packed silver kegs of beer quenched hundreds of under-aged thirsts. Even in late fall, the desert was still hot at night. The air conditioners ran continuously.

One of the young guests in her bare feet stepped in some dog doo outside. Then she stumbled into the house, tracking it onto the fluorescent carpet. Even the thick marijuana smoke filling the house could not cover the doo's distinctive odor. A crowd of disgusted visitors all pinched their noses.

"Eeeewwww!"

The drunken girl froze with embarrassment. She stood next to one of the cold kegs.

"Here. Allow me to assist."

Stewart Dawkins, a six-foot-five member of the Phoenix Jesuit Preparatory Academy crew team who had no interest in football either, grabbed the keg spout and began depressing its pump. He sprayed fresh beer on her dainty feet, washing away the dog dirt.

"It feels great!" she exclaimed.

"Happy sticky feet!" another girl shouted. "Let me try some."

She grabbed the beer hose and sprayed her bare feet. Then mayhem mixed with the beer. The crowd danced and screamed beneath a shower of sticky suds. Christine, Lucy, and Bram joined the anarchy and smiled. A stranger passed them a marijuana joint. Bram kindly demonstrated his proven methodology for smoking pot. The two girls followed his lead. In a short time, Christine, Lucy, and Bram were giggling high and drunk.

By that time the crowd had grown to several hundred high school and college-age kids as well. Moving through the packed crowd became nearly impossible. Such limited space now forced the kids to carry their plastic beer cups above their heads as not to spill them upon kind passersby. Christine's and Lucy's cheeks hurt from smiling. Their tummies hurt from laughing. Their heads spun from consuming.

Then a small herd of sticky people (including the inseparable love trio) migrated from the house out to the pool. The Mathewses had imported thousands of tiny hand-painted pool tiles from Italy, with which figures of dolphins were artistically formed—not that the hundred nude young bodies took notice. Stewart Dawkins had helped himself to Mr. Mathews's eight-millimeter reel-to-reel video camera. Stewart put to film the decadent descent. Water splashed and people howled at the waning peach-colored crescent moon above.

A stuffy conservative-minded neighbor, displeased with the infractions to local noise abatement laws coming from the Mathews mansion, called the town's police. She demanded relief, as she could no longer hear the termites eating away at her home's wooden frame. Shortly thereafter, uniformed response arrived wielding billy clubs, large hand-held lanterns, loud speaker-horns, and lethal sidearms.

Christine, Lucy, and Bram fled with haste. Lacking cognitive reasoning and basic motor skills, the love trio collected in their mobile psychedelic cocoon. Adrenaline, alcohol, and THC fueled their flight. They sped into the bite of that night. Then at Tatum ("Dead Man's") Curve, they came to a swift and unforeseen stop. All three rested quietly and bled.

The next day Karl and Capricious stood before that same crinkled psychedelic cocoon. The Valley of the Sun Auto Parts junkyard habitually assigned one of its wreckers to patrol Tatum Curve in search of "fresh kill." Capricious saw the red of the dead. Then she recognized the vehicle as Billy the Bully's sister's car. Confused and scared, she ran. Karl followed. He too knew.

Upon returning back to their neighborhood, the boy and girl saw police cruisers parked in front of both of their homes. The identifications had finally been made. The kids stopped their bikes. Hearts pounded. Knees shook. Their little bodies quivered.

Meanwhile, Billy the Bully sat on the over-seeded rye winter-blend lawn behind Paul the Border Patrol agent's house. Paul and his wife left the house on a journey to acquire baby furniture. (Paul's wife was pregnant.) Billy the Bully plopped himself just in front of Thunder's secured dog cage in the corner of the lot. He stared at the morning newspaper's headline: "Two Teens Killed in Another Dead Man's Curve Crash." His eyes and face were swollen with deep grief. His older sister, Christine, and Capricious's older sister, Lucy, had been killed. Bram clung to his life at a Phoenix hospital.

Billy inhaled from a marijuana joint that he had prepared in mourning. After suppressing for sixty seconds a cloud of carcinogens down in his lungs, he blew the smoke directly into Thunder's cage. The drug patrol dog turned enraged. It seethed with an instinct to destroy. Billy sobbed. Smoked. Then angered the dog a bit more.

Billy the Bully heard Karl and Capricious off in the short distance. Then he saw them parked in the street. He flicked the joint's hot coal into the cage at Thunder. It burned the dog's nostril and angered it even more. Billy looked at Karl. *Life was unfair. Karl's brother lived. Bram killed Christine. Karl would pay. Justice would be served.*

Billy tore down the thick string clothesline that Paul's wife used in the back of the house. He tied one end of the rope to the door latch on Thunder's cage. From within the safety of Paul's neighbor's small shed enclosure, the bully tugged at the clothesline to open the cage. Thunder stormed through the door. Karl and Capricious stood directly in the dog's line of sight. The dog caught Capricious's attractive scent and ran toward her with determined singularity.

Karl and Capricious both saw Hurricane Thunder approach. They froze. And the storm came upon them. He dove straight for Capricious. With his small might and without any fright, Karl stepped before his precious beauty to confront the great power of the beast. He loved Capricious, for it was her that broke his stuttering speech.

Karl stepped forward and raised his tiny arm into the jaws of fate. The boy amounted to only half the weight of the dog. In front of the girl, Thunder shook the boy violently from side to side. It tore his flesh. The creature separated the boy from his forearm. Capricious screamed. And then a Border Patrol Officer's bullet came into the dog's chest to put the demons down. After returning home from the mall, Border Patrol Officer Paul had emerged to end his dog Thunder's life.

* * *

Two ceiling fans squeaked. The other eight hummed and intermittently rattled as they shook. All ten were off-center and unbalanced. Their distracting characteristics threatened only the wondering minds of young blissful children seated in the wobbly pews beneath them. However precariously they spun, the fans succeeded in pushing stale air across two white and gold caskets in which Lucy's and

Christine's bodies lay. Only the sound of rustling pamphlets and weeping mourners could be heard above the creaking ceiling fans.

In the furthest back corner seat, Karl and his mother sat uncomfortably in solemn shock. Embarrassed by Bram's culpable actions the week prior, Rebekka bowed her head. Despite the shame, she had insisted on attending the funeral. She said, "It was the right thing to do." Bram lay in a hospital bed nearly dead, and Karl had lost his arm to a great Thunder-the brave boy had not fled. While one son had saved a daughter, the other had killed two. Twice widowed, Rebekka knew grief. Unto others she would not have wished such misery and disbelief.

Karl kept his head high. He observed his surroundings. To him, the flimsy church exterior stucco, thin plaster walls, cheap fans, and puny pews appeared unfitting for the loss remembered that day. Through his bandaged stump of flesh, he still felt his missing hand and fingers. Pain moved through him. With his bloodshot and tear-filled eyes, he caught the sight of his Capricious moving through the church entrance. Covered in black plumage, his dove cast upon him all the privations of her life. Empty inside, he watched her pass by. She did not notice him, her face full of swelling. Nothing glad. Karl wanted to rid her of bereavement and wipe away everything bad. If only he had. Capricious cried. That day was so sad. Karl cried. That day was so sad.

From places far, from places near, the news of these unforgettable fatalities at Dead Man's Curve brought large crowds. Many did come. They sang. Their voices echoed under a choir of perfect-pitched innocent young children and one off-tune violin-Sally Turner was not quite the music prodigy purported by her mother. Tears flowed and bells rang. *Why did this happen?* A Catholic cardinal dressed in white promised love and peace. He promoted confidence in Providence. "Never break with belief!" he said.

The children sang, "Love Reigns! Love Reigns! Love Reigns!"

Why did this happen? Capricious questioned piety's place.

Billy then stood before the living and the departed. The living leaped with Faith. The departed did nothing. He offered no hope:

Now there is nothing!
In the whole of the universe,
Now there is nothing!
All who mourn, hear this verse.
Unbroken darkness.
Endless emptiness.
Now there is nothing!
Chaos remain.

Down in unfathomable depths
Does death give me terrible pain.
No Mother Earth!
No Father Heaven!
Cruel Queen of the Underworld!
Hear me now!
Now there is nothing!
This snake sheds tears of blood.
For I am Billy.
Titan from the Sea of Revenge.
Now there is nothing!
Christine and Lucy are gone!

Billy raised his red-haired little head. No one knew that it was he who had released great Thunder upon Karl and Capricious. Writhing with pity, the mortals before him bore his burden and forgave him as quite a bit strange and all but witty.

Days later, Karl had wandered into Officer Paul's backyard. In front of Thunder's cage, he had found two cigarette butts (Billy's brand), the remains of a marijuana joint, and the slingshot that Billy had stolen from him at the pond. He realized that it had been Billy who had opened the canine's kennel. Atop the deceased dog's empty pen, Karl sat. He was tired of life and loss. Into a ball he curled and into deep sleep he passed.

Hours later in the hot afternoon, the snort and crackle of a filthy diesel truck interrupted Karl. His heavy eyelids slowed his wake. Across the street, five big moving men emerged from a dust-covered truck. For hours they cycled in and out of the Harmonys' dispirited dwelling. Moving eclectic furniture and just-packed cardboard boxes, the men removed all of the Harmonys' belongings until the house stood empty. During the process Karl had not changed his position. He watched. With each piece, deeper blue became his disposition.

The Harmony family, still wearing black and reduced in number to three, boarded themselves into their long rectangular-shaped station wagon. The car drove away. Capricious never looked back. Karl cried. For decades, he would not see her again.

FIRESTORM

DECEMBER 2009

Warm salty tears poured down C.J.'s bubbly cheeks as she sat at the finger-smudged computer monitor. She stared at the Valley of the Sun Auto Parts junkyard Internet website, remembering that thunderous day long ago. She looked down at her emerald charm bracelet. Since the moment that Karl had placed the lost bracelet on her wrist at Diamond's Department Store, C.J. had never taken it off. She read the inscription: "Happy Birthday, Lil Sis. Love U Forever.—Lucy."

C.J.'s mind paused. Her thinking of the past then came into the present. She thought about her current problem—her car. Shaking nervously, she wiped the tears away with her silk sleeve. The AM radio sports talk emanating from the other side of the house pierced through the plaster walls. The thought of Frank upset her. Desperate to get her family through this crisis, C.J. focused her keen sense. In the past, if an unscrupulous supplier had placed her public relations firm at risk, she would have immediately switched to another vendor. She remembered that she used to ship printer and copier parts in from out of state. *Why couldn't she purchase a used engine from out of state?*

Immediately she searched the Internet for used SUV engines. Engine suppliers from Texas and Tennessee boasted low miles and high quality. Then she wondered about the warranty for used engines. It did not take much further investigation for C.J. to discover that purchasing a year or two-year warranty on a used engine doubled the price of the purchase. *And how would she be able to trust a junkyard from Texas or Tennessee? They were probably as cutthroat as the local guy in Arizona. Hmm. What about a new engine from the factory in Detroit?*

In moments she found that a new engine cost only a little more than a used one with a reasonable warranty and it came with a three-year warranty. The family needed safe reliable transportation. With Frank and her both being unemployed and her money from the sale of her public relations firm being tied up in litigation, the family could not afford a new car.

The very next day C.J. rode her bike down to the mechanic.

"Good morning, pretty lady!" said good-looking Nathaniel. He leaned forward and looked down at C.J. from behind the silver-top counter. Then he clicked a pen top and popped it into his shirt pocket. With a big broad smile, he said, "Have we made a decision?"

"Yes. I called the Valley of the Sun Auto Parts junkyard."

Nathaniel stopped smiling. His eyes turned coal black.

"The used engine that you and I had discussed has ninety thousand miles on it. Its condition is unacceptable to me. He lied to you when he described it to you."

Using her savvy business acumen, C.J. knew enough not to accuse Nathaniel of attempting to cheat her. He still had her car in pieces in that back lot. She needed him to repair it. The logistics of moving the car and its pieces to another shop displeased C.J. She wanted Nathaniel to properly fix the car for a fair price.

"I called the SUV dealership just down the road from here. They have a brand new engine from the factory in stock. The dealership agreed to give you wholesale pricing. The fair retail price to me is three thousand, eight hundred dollars."

She handed Nathaniel a tiny scratch piece of paper with the dealership wholesale representative's contact information written on it.

"He's expecting your call."

"Did you purchase a long block or a short block?" Nathaniel smirked back at C.J. and leaned into her again over the counter.

Beneath her pretty curves, her body and soul buckled. She had never before heard the terms "long block" and "short block." Nathaniel grasped for an uncomfortable advantage in the negotiation. C.J. thought for a moment. Her mind raced.

"The engine is complete. The dealership advised me that the engine may only need an inexpensive grommet and should require twelve to thirteen hours of labor." She nodded her head back at him.

"You bought a long block," he stated.

C.J. smiled from ear to ear with a grin the size of the Grand Canyon. She stood proud in the face of adversity.

"Tell you what," replied Nathaniel. "I'll call the dealership today and give you a ring at your home to confirm everything. We'll take care of you and your car."

C.J. knew that if she had not researched the details of the engine, Nathaniel would have overcharged her for unneeded parts and labor. She spun around on her tiptoes and skipped out of the store.

On the bike ride home, she could not pedal fast enough. She fantasized about Karl riding ahead of her on his Blue Flame bicycle. It felt wonderful to have him in the lead. In her vivid imagination, she felt so comfortable riding under his wing. He smelled clean. He looked powerful.

Then she stopped suddenly and came back into the present. *The shop had to get the new engine installed into the SUV. Were those grimy guys capable of accomplishing such a huge job? How often does a shop install a new engine? Nobody was crazy enough to buy a new engine. Most people just purchased another car! Maybe this was a mistake.*

"Good day, ma'am," greeted Bob a few days later. All the other oil-covered employees at the shop knew she had arrived. They pointed their soot-stained faces toward her. White-eyes glowed. The tall owner of the family-owned business came out through a door hanging on its frame by only a single hinge. She paid a fair price for the towing, the parts, and the labor; for all that was done. Six mechanics including Nathaniel and the proprietor escorted C.J. out to her car. She gasped when she saw that they had taken the extra time to wash and wax her baby. With pride the men formed a half circle around her wagon. They had polished the tires and vacuumed the interior. It looked almost new.

"We haven't done one of these installs in a while. Here is a bag of leftover parts," said Nathaniel.

C.J. stood expressionless. The circle of not too many paused. Then roared with laughter.

"Gotcha!"

She laughed with relief.

"Ma'am, we did a complete diagnostic and everything is running perfect. We are very confident that she'll run just fine like a top. That little knock you hear is just a pulley in the power steering mechanism. Nothing serious. To be expected on a car with one hundred and fifty thousand miles on it. Of course, you know the long block did not include the power steering mechanism. We'd like you to come back in a little while after you have driven a thousand miles on her so we can double-check everything and give you an oil change on the house. If there are any adjustments needed, we'll take care of them. Here are the keys and the engine warranty certificate. She's as good as new!"

C.J. was so immensely happy. She beamed as she drove away. The mechanics had been kind enough to help her load her bicycle into the back of the SUV. They treated her like a lady, and she appreciated the gentlemen for their extra effort.

Overcome with excitement and relief on the trip home, she parked the car in a grocery store lot just to listen to her new engine purr. She did it! She did it! She did it!

She saved her car. From her purse she tore a small clean white sheet from a tiny memo pad. Grabbed a pen and wrote:

> Karl,
>
> I am at a crossroads in my life. I think we should discuss over coffee.
>
> Capricious

* * *

Days later Karl waited. He sat in an uncomfortable creaky chair within the walls of a quaint coffee shop. Every woman he had ever known had always kept him waiting. He loved to wait for a woman, especially his Capricious. The anticipation grew with every painful moment. As other coffee aficionados nervously waited in line for their caffeine fix, Karl itched for his "fix." He wondered what she would be wearing. Her outfits always expressed so much style and confidence.

At times Karl reacted to ambling passersby staring at his prosthetic right forearm. Though he had gotten used to the gawking, he often wore long sleeves, even in hot weather. His stunning good looks and impeccable taste in fine tailored clothing usually attracted eyes away from his arm. However, sometimes an inconspicuous observer would force Karl to raise an eyebrow and flex his chest. He would use his mechanical hand to raise his coffee cup to his mouth while winking at an onlooker. His smooth methodology always won him favor. Embarrassed in response, those who ogled usually looked to the ground as if a hundred dollar bill lay between their feet.

Every time the coffee shop entrance door flew open and dinged, a spike of sharp emotion cut through Karl. Such jolts paralyzed him momentarily. Then he remembered his precious cargo riding at the bow of his *Goodyear Frogger*. He thought about nudging her with his perfect push stick through the Port of Lilies as paradise parted around her silhouette.

Karl reached into his pocket and withdrew C.J.'s note that she had written to him. He read it over and over again. Her voice rang in his ears as he read. The words permanently etched themselves into his feelings. And then it came to him. When she arrived, he believed that day would be the very day that their lifelong passion would come to fruition. It was inevitable.

Karl began plotting and planning the seduction. Capricious and he would forever erase the mild desert winter with their firestorm of heat. They might hold hands under the coffee table. Their knees would touch. Her toe would find its way under his pants cuff. He would move into her and feel her breath. *Would the crowd be gawking then?*

Karl could not wait to feel her skin and her pulse. Both of them would fear discovery. Maybe he would invite her to come with him back to Farmers Pond.

Karl decided that he would wait for five more minutes. And wait five more...

* * *

Against the descending flight of silver-haired "snowbirds" driving south in classic cars with white-walled tires, Karl escorted his Capricious north. Out of the mild seventy-degree January desert valley weather, the two "lovebirds" ascended. Burdened by guilt, they flapped their heavy wings toward Flagstaff's snow-covered pine-topped mountains just below the Grand Canyon. The crack in the car's window permitted fresh chilled air to tickle their scalps. Goose bumps.

As they traveled north along their secret sojourn, the Arizona foliage gradually turned from sundried dead to plush forest green-alive. They drove past sonorous red rock walls echoing T.C. Schebly's ghost proclaiming never-ending love to his wife, Sedona. Then the snowline, a low cloud ceiling, limited visibility, and a large twelve-point elk crossing the freeway welcomed the two. In the dense grey blizzard, eighteen-wheelers and family passenger cars slipped off the slick roadway into soft windblown drifts of otherwise fluffy fun. The salt trucks had not yet come, and the Arizona Department of Safety closed the roads behind them.

Cut off from the valley below, Karl led his lady astray. Capricious smiled, wide-eyed and ruby cheeked. A little nervous, she grabbed Karl's forearm as he drove. She had forgotten his prosthetic state. Her palm fused with his cold metal arm. Though she craved the touch of his flesh, she found comfort in the steel symbol of his heroism. In the frigidity of the moment, both forgot their lives and set free their forbidden love. Liberty. Karl looked at Capricious. Her emotions unfettered, she opened her heart to him. His eyes glazed over with tears.

The moment passed and he returned his compass back to navigating the treacherous conditions outside. He drove her to a clandestine cedar-planked cabin, elevation eight thousand feet high. They snuggled on a cozy fur-covered floor in front of a crackling glow. A hot fire gently cast flickering shadows across their middle-aged wisdom and foolish young-spirited vim.

Capricious asked, "Why?"

"Don't think about it."

"Karl, we could have had a life together. Why didn't our paths cross sooner? Why?"

"I looked for you in crowds," he said in his taming low tone.

They embraced. The heat of fire radiated the side of Capricious's face. King Hoogeveen heated her heart. "Oh, Karl," she whispered. He held her tightly against his muscular chest. *If only it would never end.* Karl grabbed the back of her arm. Moved his hand to the pretty flesh under her shoulder blade. Squeezed. His knee encroached between hers. Capricious parted. Her eyes were half closed in the thin mountain air. Her hunk nuzzled her cinnabar hair. He exposed all her fantastic female senses-safe and secure, her feelings so bare. Karl watched his love slip easily into perfect slumber. A gentleman was he. The gentleman waited.

Drained, they both fell back into a bundle of wool blankets and fell fast asleep in each other's arms.

Scents of faint smolder, woodsy pine, and maple-flavored bacon woke Capricious. Karl whistled while he worked in the cabin's cute yellow kitchen. His hair disheveled and his shirt not tucked, Capricious had never seen her precise prince free from smear and free from speck. Cured strips of pork splattered. Bread toasted. Eggs scrambled. Grape jelly jammed. "I love you," Karl wanted to say. Karl and Capricious were happy that day.

With full bellies the two boarded a red and yellow trolley headed for fun. Wrapped in matching new ski outfits, they bumped and jiggled. The bus wiggled. They tightly held bright-colored skis and dark-colored poles. Everything jolly. Finally the vehicle stopped. Off they jumped into a blinding blanket of white. Their folly never dropped.

Armed with two expensive "All Mountain" passes, Karl and Capricious wore stylish glasses. Across the bottom plain they gracefully skated, unencumbered by skis that to others proved awkward. For a few minutes they waited in line, scooting forward four people at a time. The "quad" chairlift scooped up every passenger-ready or not. The longhaired operator watched the calamity. He never intervened. The helpless clumsy beginners thickened the chairlifting heart-stopping plot. *Every man, woman, and child for himself!* Seated on the silent moving lift, Karl and Capricious looked up at the grey sky. Big snowflakes quietly pummeled their runny noses, each with a dash of frosty splash. The two snickered with glee. Dangling from green branches, college girls' pink undergarments decorated each winter tree. More smiles. More fun.

Off in the distance, great spiral-horned mountain goats marched up to the formidable steep peak. Then Karl swiftly led Capricious on to their first ski run. She followed him left. She followed him right. He danced through powered moguls. Behind him, she pranced through his trail of powdered sugar. In his shadow she forever wished to be. Capricious chased Karl up and down the mountain that dreamy winter day. The two hoped they could stay.

* * *

...And the predator of passion pounced upon his prey with indomitable force. Her flesh melted beneath him. To her delight, he extorted every tension in her soul. By this brute force, her loneliness departed her, and she felt safe beneath him. He looked deeply into the sparkle of her zircon eyes and gnawed on her delicate shoulder. She acquiesced to his grace and power. As her body clenched uncontrollably around her attacker, she left the moment. Into a new wonderful world this giant gently placed his willing fawn. The loving continued until dawn.

Gale

Sixty-year-old Bram arrived at Karl's house wearing overly weathered waffle-bottom sneakers, tattered trousers, and an oil-stained shirt. Responding to the ding of the doorbell, Karl opened the entrance to his home. He greeted his brother with anything but glee. Bram's ugly attire simply could not be. Primed and polished was Karl's decree. To the Snake Pit Cabaret they intended to flee.

Karl fitted Bram with a hundred-sixty thread count, moon-colored shirt, and a swanky pair of khaki pressed pants to match. Then readied, they headed up north, where men played and later denied every sin. Upon winding dirt switchbacks, the crew of two pursued one night of fun. They passed coyotes, kit fox, a mountain lion, four desert cottontail, and a barn owl peering down on them from above.

Finally Karl's dust-covered SUV bounced to a stop. The car killed a little lizard under a lunar glow. To the right, a bevy of baby boomer motorcycles, all shiny and bright, packed much of the lot. The cabaret's flickering neon lights blinded Karl's and Bram's squinting sight. The smell of sticky stale spirits, baby powder perfume, and a collection of caged live lizards teased these merry men into this scary den.

A twenty-dollar cover fee, a sign kindly requesting all freedom-loving patriots to check all sidearms, and a tall, pale, redheaded Scotsman called Angry quelled any spite. *Thump. Thump. Thump.* The music drowned them with deafening decibels. Into the Pit they descended. Purple, blue, and pink stage lights flashed and spun over the conditioned crowd. Topless beauties tamed them into submissive smiles. The men's yellow teeth lit up with the florescent stage light reflection. Prancing women, tall and straight, towered over the desperate souls huddled on low velvet sofas. Some served them overpriced suds and prodded them to swill plenty more.

Beaming handsome Karl and worn-down Bram cut through the crowd and its tacit capacity for groveling. They stepped up to the bar and met their mates, Colonel Wiley, Retired, Mr. Andersen, and Mr. Florence from the Rancho Opulente neighborhood. Two pretty bartenders dressed in black leather and a third dressed in white lace convened around a glass-windowed refrigerator. A long, thick, Burmese python pet had wrapped itself into the coils behind the refrigerated beer storage unit. In keeping with the club's theme, a hundred or more caged exotic snakes lined the walls of the Snake Pit Cabaret. One of them (if not more?) had escaped. Seeking the heat of the coils, the cold-blooded python twisted itself around the warm metal. Six able hands tugged and tugged to unwind the snake. In fifteen minutes time, the trio unwrapped the unhappy varmint before he could snap at them with a bite.

Karl, the colonel, and the rest of the thirsty patrons watched the three unravel the mess with a little bit of fright.

"I don't like snakes," Bram said.

"Women and snakes turn me on!" the colonel replied.

"I gotta snake for those girls right here." Small Mr. Andersen boasted what little he could provide.

"Bull. Who you kiddin'?" The colonel jabbed. "Even if you had the chance, you wouldn't touch those girls. Your wife has you wrapped around her finger!"

"Hey. Divorce is bad business. I know too many guys livin' on half their income. And I'm a big money guy. Nobody is gettin' half o' mine."

"Well, if your situation should change, call me," said Mr. Florence. He handed Mr. Andersen his attorney of law business card.

"'Divorces and Bankruptcies!'" Mr. Andersen laughed. "You must be making a killing nowadays during this damned recession."

I'm gettin' married." A young man standing at the bar next to the gents from Opulente spoke up.

The crew said nothing. They sat silently contemplating the prospect of this man's demise.

"No, you're not. Tell us you're not getting married."

"Yea. Yea. I'm getting married."

"Well. Say good-bye to your money and your friends. You're done!"

The college-aged kid stood silent.

"Why? Lemme ask you. Why?" Mr. Andersen perked up.

"Well, I guess I love 'er."

"Bull! Love ain't got nothin' to do with it. Why are you getting married?"

"Well. Uh. I guess because I don't want to lose 'er."

"Aha!"

"She's forcing you into it!"

The kid turned pale. The crowd roared with laughter.

"Don't worry, kid," said smooth Mr. Florence. "It's not so bad. Don't let these guys scare you. Marriage is great. I for one am very happy."

Mr. Florence had much for which to be thankful. His wife and he had gotten along quite well for quite a spell. With each other they flirted obsessively.

"Bologna! He's lyin'!" said Mr. Andersen.

"No, I'm not lying. I am happy. Lemme give you a little advice, kid. Everybody says women are a mystery. Lemme tell ya. They're not. Women are attracted to power. Find your power and with it—lead the family. You wear the pants. I'm not talking about being a jerk. Leadership, respect, and trust are things you have to earn. You can't demand it. I am talking about being strong and decisive. Listen and accept her input on things. I mean really listen. But in the end, you make the call on the big stuff and stand behind your decision. Don't ever blame her for stuff. Never point the finger. If she is to blame, she'll know it. No need for you to verbalize it. No need for you to stick her nose in it. That doesn't mean you let her push you around. You are the pack leader. Stand firm and establish boundaries. The way to mold her into your boundaries is by paying attention to her. Be involved in her daily life. Appeal to her complexities and sensitivities. You ever notice that women pick shampoo by the smell? She sees and feels the world in a very different way than you do."

"You got that right!" the colonel butted in.

"I am serious. She processes information in a much more sophisticated manner than we do. Not only does she interpret the raw facts and data like we do, but she also processes other input according to her senses—the sounds, the smells, the way something feels to the touch. She is in tune with the feelings of everybody around her. She thinks about all of this stuff as it is happening in the moment. To us, all that stuff clogs up our brains and gives us a confusing headache. She is, on the other hand, interpreting all of it."

"Bull. All that stuff just makes her confused and unable to make decisions," the colonel retorted.

Mr. Florence continued. "In a way, that is where we can help. Be involved in her decision. We can help her sort through it all and help her feel confident in the final decision. That is the support we can give. It also gives her confidence that her role in the family is important. Which, as we all know, is important. Admit it, colonel."

The colonel sat silent.

"Come on. Admit it."

"OK. I agree. Our wives are important."

"Absolutely. Imagine our lives without our wives. Not a pretty picture."

"But I still don't go to the mall unless it's a special guest appearance to make a decision on a big purchase," said the colonel.

"I love to go to the mall," declared Mr. Florence. "To me it's a chance to show off my family—my greatest pride—to the rest of the world, especially other women. I love getting looks from other 'hotties' at the mall while my wife is looking through the clothes rack. I am proud of her and my kids. It's great."

"You're weird. I'd rather be watching the game on TV."

"I am tellin' you. If you give just a little bit each day, she returns the favor a hundred times back. I take a few minutes out of every day to call my wife to ask her about her day. If she's at work or at the store, I'll ask details about what she's doing. And I listen."

Bachelor Bram, who had heard enough, stepped up from the bar and walked over to "The Confessional." It offered club patrons the opportunity to confess their sins to an unsympathetic dominatrix wearing thigh-high studded leather boots. Bram had something to confess.

Karl also excused himself from the bar and the Opulente discourse. In a dark corner, he thought of C.J. He looked at the Gaboon viper snake staring coldly at him through the aquarium glass. Karl cowered into the velvet couch. He hated snakes too. Conflicted, he thought of Capricious, his wife, and his kids.

At the backside of the establishment, Bram knelt down before Gale the dominatrix.

"Forgive me, Mistress, for I have sinned."

"How long has it been since your last confession?" She lightly smacked him on the head with a leather-horsewhipping strap.

"This is my first confession."

"'This is my first confession, Mistress,'" she demanded and smacked him again. "Confess your sins," she ordered.

"Mistress, do you believe it's possible to love two women equally at the same time?"

Smack. She hit him harder.

"Continue, you sorry pig."

"Mistress, I loved two at once. And it was wonderful."

Bram paused. Looked up at her.

"Don't look at me."

Smack.

"You ever been in love, Mistress?"

Smack. Then she smiled as she thought about it. "This isn't about me," she said.

Smack.

"As I said, Mistress...It was absolutely wonderful. My first and only 'two-love.' Ah, the three of us; we were inseparable. We went everywhere together. We laughed together. We cried together. We had so much fun together. Every moment was so precious. We shared so many intense emotions."

"So what happened? What do you have to confess?" She examined the scars covering the exposed skin on his face and arms, remnants of the accident at Dead Man's Curve.

* * *

Almost forty years earlier on the night of Marsha Mathews's big party in Paradise Valley, Bram had persuaded Christine and Lucy to abandon the plans to attend the rivalry high school football game in favor of intoxicating mania at a mansion. When the cops came, Christine, Lucy, and Bram fled the fun. Into the psychedelic van they ran. As always, Christine took the helm, Bram navigated, and Lucy sat in the backseat.

Toward the bend in Tatum Road, they drove. Down. Down. Down. Was this true love? Fearing capture and conviction, Bram's adrenaline pumped. He could feel the tip of his hair and the outer layer of his eyeballs. For Bram, Christine could not drive fast enough.

"Christine! Faster! Faster!" he shouted.

But she would not go. Christine was too slow. Handsome Bram could not see Tatum Bend ahead and below. He only wanted the car to go. Christine was too slow. Bram encroached upon the pilot's command. He stepped on the accelerator atop Christine's delicate foot. In silence they sped. Down. Down. Down. They did not negotiate Tatum Bend. Over the curb and through the air, they sped. The van spun and spun. No one screamed. Only silence prevailed. Newtonian laws of physics intervened. Nature's centrifugal force ejected three bodies from the rotating van. Then the van and the trio returned to earth with a crash, a crush, and a tumble.

In moments Bram awoke from his traumatic slumber. He and his first "two-love" lay in a bed of blooming beavertail cactus. Christine had been decapitated. Her body rested peacefully in the flowering magenta cactus. Bram looked into Lucy's eyes. They too lay among the beautiful magenta. Bram could feel the hundreds of hair-thin cactus needles piercing his flesh. Lucy could feel nothing. Her neck had been broken in seven places, paralyzing her. She could only blink her eyes. Beneath the moonlight she looked at Bram. She couldn't even cry. She didn't know why.

Together they remained there, suffering. Help was on the way, but not soon enough. Bram could not move his broken body. He watched Lucy. Listened to her breathing become shallower in the night.

"Oh, Bram," she said. Then she quietly eased away into God's forgiving hands.

* * *

Bram opened his eyes after confessing his story. Mistress Gale stood silently in tears before him. It surprised him to see her express emotion. She had difficulty composing herself.

"They convicted me," he said. "I told them that I drove. That it was my fault. I spent twelve years in jail."

She said nothing. Did not know what to say. She was shocked and depressed. Then she became angry. She yelled, "I am going to tear your flesh. Bend over."

Mistress Gale proceeded to paddle fifty times his bare bottom. But she could injure him no more. He never fully recovered from his forty-year-old injuries. Chronic depression and illness characterized the remainder of his life.

Outside, the entire world shook as the distinctive thunder of many custom motorcycles approached. *Blub. Blub. Blub. Blub. Blub. Blub.* The Sidewinders bellicose biker organization had come home to roost at *their* Snake Pit. Conspicuously marked with varietal tattoos originating from penitentiaries near and far, the ruffians unsettled the dust upon their arrival. The establishment immediately closed. As the stampeding herd of patrons fled with haste, a pair of other motorcycles made their way up toward the parking lot against the crowd. Each of those two iron ponies differed from the others. Upon the dull white 1958 classic named Storm rode a huge red-haired bearded man—Bull (Billy the Bully)—six feet ten, weighing almost four hundred pounds, wearing a leather vest with a three-piece gang patch on the back. Years of riding appeared to have weathered the symbols sown into the front of the vest. Barely able to wrap her arms and legs around his massive trunk, a tall muscular blonde clung to him. She wore a three-piece property patch. Her shapely tanned leg served as a canvas for the long red, green, orange, yellow, and blue ink dragon tattoo needled into her skin.

To their left a lanky crustacean hid in Bull's shadow. Bull's wingman, Spiny, rode on the bike behind Bull. Spiny sat upon a bright red Fat Bob with a suicide shift. As they stopped, he struggled to maintain the bike's balance as he rested it on the kickstand and shut off its engine. These reborn children of Christ wore proudly their "AZ Bikers for Jesus" patches on the backs of their vests. With a Bible in his hand and a lofty mission of salvation on his mind, Bull entered the Pit by himself.

THE DESERT ANGLER

JANUARY 2010

Three days later the rising sun pierced through an opening in a set of blinds located on an Opulente cul-de-sac. The sun heated the colonel's wife's heavy eyelids. But it did not wake her from deep slumber. Her drunken eyes had glued themselves shut through the night. She did not have the strength to open her eyes to greet the day. Neither she nor her teenagers would wake for several hours.

Colonel Wiley did not mind. In fact, he preferred it that way. He owned the mornings. The colonel had risen hours earlier. Alcohol never prevented him from an early-morning rise. He had already made the coffee, read the sports page, smoked five cigarettes, and had begun planning his day. He only then noticed the newspaper headline.

* * *

Two beer-fisted fishermen sat shoreside Rancho Opulente's small man-made pond. They eagerly baited farm-raised largemouth bass and rainbow trout swimming at the bottom while young eager boys dipped their poles too. The pond, stocked monthly by the community association, represented a spit to some; but to these few— an ocean. One of the two, Harry, once again with his fluorescent fishing line, painted fluid patterns above the slightly rippled water and gently placed on the pond's surface the fly tied at the line's end. He let the fluffy fly rest a beat and a half to a melodic rhythm before he whipped it up and let it glide fro. Then to again. The artistic metronome became a soulful silent tune against a slight nippy breeze. With the suddenness of a phonograph needle skipping off a plastic record disc, Harry's symphony halted. He pulled and tugged at a heavyweight dragging his line. The pond shore-men laughed. They jumped up. They jumped down. For the great fly fisherman Harry snagged a large "tree bass." Two children joined Harry in the slow fight. They hoped to land a worthless piece of dud. The shape came closer, barely afloat. It looked like a log no more. The jokes then turned to terror there in the outdoor.

The headline later read: "Man Found Dead in Rancho Opulente Pond." Harry the Fisherman had reeled in a body—Bull the Storm Rider's body, Billy the Bully's body. The initial report surmised that a Gaboon viper had bitten Bull; that the venomous bite had caused him to bleed profusely from every orifice of his big body; that he bled painfully and slowly to death. Bull had been dead for three days, floating in the pond just beneath Rainbow Rapids.

* * *

"Strategic foreclosure!" Colonel Wiley did say. "I'm walkin' away," he proclaimed to Karl without any dismay. The two spoke in front of Bram's shiny moving van sparkling in the break of an Arizona winter day.

"I think since home prices have tanked, the house lost about half a million bucks. Makes no sense to stay in the thing."

"You refinanced and took all the money out of the house when prices rose?" Karl asked.

"Of course! Didn't you? Everybody was doin' it. If a tree gives you fruit, you pick it. If it stops giving, cut it down. Who cares? I don't know anybody who didn't take money out of their house."

There had already been far too many foreclosures in the neighborhood. Karl boiled inside, knowing the "strategic foreclosure" would only push neighborhood home prices even further down. He said nothing and gritted his teeth.

"Say, uh, you mind coming into the house for a few minutes? My swordfish needs taken down. I like that handled first before the other furniture. Priorities, my friend!"

"Sure. No problem."

After the Rainbow Rapids company had closed its doors forever, Karl had split his time between maintaining Opulente's artificial river, raising Arizona King Crab in his house, and helping his brother with the moving company. As Karl walked into the colonel's home, he noticed the sheriff's bank foreclosure sticker posted on the front door. The sight repulsed Karl.

Inside the colonel's home, the colonel asked, "You think you can remove it?" He stood looking up at the crooked swordfish drooping from the wall. Karl nodded. "So how'd ya' lose your arm?" the colonel continued.

Karl ignored him. Returned to the truck and came back with an eighteen-foot-high ladder. With grace and skill he easily positioned the long length of steps just beneath the great plastic fish above him. "Lightning," the swordfish, reminded him of the first day he saw C.J. standing with the other ladies in front of the colonel's home. He remembered her Sedona-red lips and her cinnabar curls. Karl thought back to their childhood—to stealing soda pop and killing frogs aboard the *Goodyear Frogger*. He thought back to the day he voiced his first word to her—to the feeling of being able to speak after years of silence. And of the essence of being able to communicate with another human being for the first time, that he felt so calm and confident when he stood with her. She liberated him. Even then beneath the fish, Karl could feel the tickle of her curls upon his nose, when as a child, he had whispered his name in her ear. A chill ran through him. He could feel her within him. Suddenly his guilt lifted. He realized that he, Karl Hoogeveen, loved Capricious J. Harmony. He would tell the world, and he would end this desperate torment. C.J. and Karl would be together, as it should be.

With C.J. on his mind and a broad smile upon his face, Karl ascended the ladder to take down the fish. With one great hand upon its tail, he adjusted its angle upon the hooks drilled into the wall. He jerked and he tugged. He poked and he pulled. Then "Lightning" struck.

The whale of a fish crashed down upon him. It consumed him into its belly. Karl the Jonah remained in its stomach for what seemed like three days and three nights. Then the fish spit Karl, and a great holy spirit appeared before him. Bull the Storm Rider called his name.

"K-K-K-Karl," said Bull's ghost.

Karl remained stunned in silence.

"K-K-K-Karl."

"Who are you?" asked Karl.

"You Knu-Knu-Knu-Knucklehead! You're a stuttering idiot, you fool."

"What?"

"Do you know the Book of Genesis? The story of Creation?"

"No," Karl replied grimly.

"In the beginning the earth was without form and without shape. On the first day God said, 'Let there be light.' And there was light. He saw that light was good and separated the light from darkness. God called the light 'Day' and the darkness 'Night.' On the second day, God separated the sky above from the water below and on the third day, God said, 'Let there be land.' He separated land from water and created plants and trees. On the fourth day, God made the moon and the sun and stars. He put them into the sky. On the fifth day, God said, 'Let there be an abundance of creatures in the sea and let there be creatures that fly in the sky.' He said, 'Let them multiply.'

On the sixth day, God said, 'Let there be every kind of wild animal to roam the land.' He saw that it was good and he made man and woman in his likeness. He blessed them and gave them dominion over everything he had created. God saw that his creation was good. On the seventh day, he rested."

Karl sighed.

"Karl, we are all instruments of God living in his image beneath his light. I ask you, man. Are you living in his likeness and in his light? Are you casting his shadow upon the earth, or are you casting your own shadow?"

"Uh. I dunno." Karl could not look Bull in the eye.

"Karl, you are fleeing from the Lord. Rancho Opulente flees from the Lord. Through his divine right to punish, God is sending a great storm. Scorpions will follow grasshoppers into your attics, and the scorpions will rain down upon your children through ceiling air vents. Vast sinkholes in the earth will consume your cars and your homes. Arizona will no longer be the Grand Canyon State. It will be the Grand Sinkhole State. West Nile disease and valley fever will inflict the young and the old. The poor Mexican kids from the Phoenix *barrio* with their unselfish artistic style of play will pounce your premier soccer team and their horrendous long balls to the corner of the pitch. Great sandstorms higher than Mount Everest's elevation will rage through Rancho Opulente. Your divine mission, Karl, is to warn Rancho. God commands you all to repent. Nineveh needs you, man. Your family needs you. Don't turn your back on them. The Lord commands you to do what is right. Go to her!"

"Bull, you took my right arm," replied Karl.

"God works in mysterious ways. You saved Capricious from Hurricane Thunder. Now go save Nineveh and Opulente from God's wrath. Go, man!"

Karl blinked, and Bull disappeared.

"Karl! Karl! You OK?" said the colonel.

"Huh?"

"You're quite the desert angler. Caught yourself a mighty fish!"

"You believe in God?" Karl uttered these rare precious words without stuttering.

"What are you talkin' about, boy?"

"Do you believe in God?" asked Karl. The colonel looked at Karl with a blank stare.

"God came to me. I saw God."

"I dunno about you seein' God, kid. That religious stuff is *Bull!*"

"I am sorry about the fish," said Karl. The great fish lay in pieces.

"Well, I guess the fish wasn't meant to be, kid. Wasn't meant to be."

Karl and his small crew returned to packing full the moving truck with the Wileys' furniture. The truck departed. Bram drove and Karl rode in the passenger seat, staring out into the changed world around him. C.J. stood in her driveway as Karl passed. They looked into each other's eyes. As C.J. left his soul, forbidden love tore their hearts for the last time. Karl waved good-bye. Both would return to quiet lives of proud parenting. From behind C.J., her husband, Frank, yelled to her and said, "Honey! I cleaned the cat litter box."

Then the Wiley family drove through Rancho Opulente one final time. They passed home after home decorated with foreclosure stickers. In their pearl-colored SUV, they sped by the pond—the ocean to some. Two beer-fisted fishermen sat shore-side watching them pass. With one finger the colonel spun the driver's wheel left and leaned into a turn leading out of the neighborhood under the falling sun. Behind them, it dropped into the rigid horizon, temporarily giving a sparkling array of orange, purple, and pink color to the otherwise brown desert beneath it. The day was done.

www.ingramcontent.com/pod-product-compliance
Lightning Source LLC
Chambersburg PA
CBHW070837280626
47161CB00015B/1029